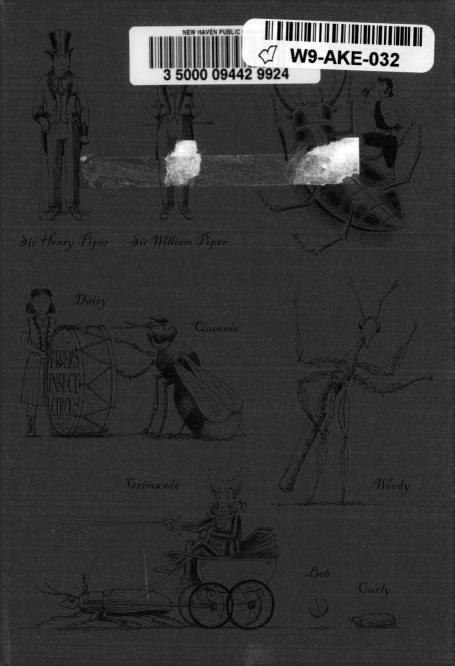

Sir Henry Piper   Sir William Piper

Daisy

Queenie

PIPERS
INSECT
CIRCUS

Woody

Grimwade

Bob

Curly

The Bundle at
BLACKTHORPE
· · · · · HEATH · · · · ·

The Bundle at
BLACKTHORPE
HEATH

◆ • • • • ◆ • • • • ◆

·· MARK ··
COPELAND

Houghton Mifflin Company Boston 2006

www.houghtonmifflinbooks.com

The text of this book is set in 11-point Legacy.
The illustrations were done in dip pen and ink.

Library of Congress Cataloging-in-Publication Data
Copeland, Mark, 1956–
The bundle at Blackthorpe Heath / written and illustrated by Mark Copeland.
p. cm.
Summary: Twelve-year-old Art, with the help of a ladybug named Rufus,
uncovers a fly's plot to ruin his family's traveling insect circus.
ISBN 0-618-56302-4 (hardcover)
[1. Circus—Fiction. 2. Insects—Fiction. 3. Family—Fiction.] I. Title.
PZ7.C7886Bun 2006   [Fic]—dc22   2005025443

ISBN-13: 978-0618-56302-9

Book design by Maryellen Hanley

Manufactured in the United States of America
HAD 10 9 8 7 6 5 4 3 2 1

ACKNOWLEDGMENTS

I would like to give a round of applause to Jess Wilder, of Portal Gallery, London, for persuading me to paint the exhibition of insect circus pictures that Robin Bugbee came upon as he strolled through Mayfair in May 2002.

I raise the roof and throw my hat in the air as high as I can for Robin for being so enthused by the show that he encouraged me to write this story, be my agent, and find a publisher.

Four cheers for Sam Byers, Richard Byers, Amanda Hodgkinson, and Fraser Harrison, who recommended, facilitated, flattered, and helped me go in a forward direction.

An intermission ice cream for my parents, Pauline and Douglas Copeland, for their support.

Hip-hip-hip-hooray for Kate O'Sullivan, my editor at Houghton Mifflin, for sympathetically corralling my wayward words.

A bow, and a nod, to all at the Insect Circus Society (of Great Britain) for providing the source material.

And a trumpet fanfare, a one-man Mexican wave, and a weevil whistle to my wife, Sarah Munro (without whom I would have achieved very little).

The Bundle at
BLACKTHORPE
· · · · · · HEATH · · · · ·

MY TWELFTH BIRTHDAY, IN THE JUNE of that long hot summer, was a day I will never forget. Among the many wondrous presents I received, Daisy gave me a small jewel-framed signaling mirror and from Grimwade the clown came a handwritten booklet entitled *Sharpen Your Skittling Skills, the Grimwade Way*. "I know it's good," he told me proudly, "because I wrote it myself." But the very best gift of all was from my grandfather, the great insect circus ringmaster Sir Henry Piper. He presented me with a beautiful brass spyglass, and I do firmly believe that had he not, my grandfather and I would have met our doom within the week.

"Art," he said to me in his slow, deep voice, "you look after this here telescopic eyepiece. In former times, it belonged to your great-grandfather, George, the founder of our illustrious traveling circus, and it's a fine and an ancient instrument. You must use it only for purposes that are to the good, for it would not be wise, and I have not given it to you, to go spying upon your friends and neighbors, as you may see things that could lead you into trouble. Instead, it is for your greater enjoyment of the wonders of the sky at night."

Well, I was as happy as a bug in butter, for I was fond of staring up into the night sky. I took great pleasure in observing the Milky Way and tracing the constellations with my outstretched finger: the Great Snail; Picus, the Water Beetle; the Nymph; and all the rest. My favorite was the Great Snail as, unlike most boys of my age, I had a great snail of my own to care for. Her name was Sylvia and, as well as dancing nightly in our mighty circus, she pulled our family caravan from town to town to the performance ground that is known in circus circles as the tober.

My bed was high up in the rafters of my family's

caravan, in the roof space called the mollycroft, and I would often lie awake for hours looking out the little windows at the starry sky. On especially mild nights Daisy and I, with my trusty pet ladybug, Rufus, for company, were allowed to sleep outdoors all tucked up between the caravans and the fire, viewing the stars above.

Daisy was the daughter of Chester Cheyne, the circus bandmaster. She was a most accomplished bareback beetle rider, and her act was one of the highlights of the show. As Sorrel, her trusty steed, raced around the ring, Daisy would balance upon Sorrel's back, skipping and jumping through a hoop.

She was my closest friend, for we had grown up together. When we arrived at a new tober we would arrange to have our caravans parked in view of each other. Daisy slept in the mollycroft of her own family's wagon, and over the years we had devised a system of signaling to each other from our beds using mirrors. We flashed the reflected light of the moon back and forth between us, using an alphabetic code of our own invention.

The night of my birthday party was clear but cold, and since we could not sleep out under the stars we retired to our beds. When I wished Daisy good night, she said to me with a smile, "Now, you're not to go spying on me in my sleep through your new telescope, Art, for that wouldn't be right and proper."

"I never would," I answered her honestly, for it had not even occurred to me to do so.

Up in my bed I signaled a good night to Daisy with the new mirror she had given to me, and she wished me the same in return.

I looked again through all my wonderful presents until I came to the spyglass. It was made of fine brass tubing, and when outstretched it was as long as my arm but when pushed closed it could fit neatly into my pocket. I pulled it open and trained it on the sky above. What sights met my eye! The stars with which I was familiar shone so brightly, I could barely look at them, and thousands upon thousands of new wonders were made visible to me.

As I traced the glittering outline of the Great Snail's shell, a fiery shooting star came into view. Following its downward trail I saw it drop behind a wood, where, to my surprise, a strange sight lay before me. There at the base of a tall tree, some way down the lane, our Agent in Advance, Seth Midden (as common a fly as you can imagine), was in conversation with another fly and a menacing black and yellow creature. I knew it could be nothing other than a wasp!

Now, a wasp was a creature that I had never seen before, but I had heard many tales of their evil temper and I knew that a sting from one could prove fatal. I also knew that it was unwise to mention wasps in Grandfather's company, as he would fly into a great rage and cuss, complaining of how they had been the cause of the breakup of the great Piper Family Circus.

So this was a most curious thing: our trusted agent in company with a wasp. I determined to keep a watchful eye on Seth, as I feared that he was up to no good.

With my eye still fixed to my telescope, I looked to see if Daisy was awake, for I wanted to share with her what I had just seen. The walls around her bed were covered with colorful rosettes and pictures of famous circus beetles and their riders, and as I ranged across them Daisy's face suddenly filled the spyglass. She blushed and looked very cross and in an instant pulled her curtains closed.

So, this is how I am ashamed to say that I took to using my spyglass for spying, and Grandfather was most certainly right, for a whole mess of trouble is what I got into.

CHAPTER 2

ITT WAS THE AGENT IN ADVANCE'S JOB TO
travel ahead of the circus to find tobers and make
arrangements for water and provision for the animals and such. He was also responsible for hanging
posters around the towns and villages in advertisement
of the forthcoming attraction. The success or failure of
a touring circus depended on the cunning and skill of
its agent.

Since the early days of the traveling insect shows, it
has been the practice to employ flies for this purpose.
They are active, hardworking creatures, and although
they are not sociable apart from with their own kind,
they love nothing better than the sights and smells of
the circus environment.

As there is an intense rivalry between traveling circuses, so there is between agents. And if rival flies happen upon each other on the road, a bundle is certain to ensue. Therefore, one of Seth's principal jobs was to spy out other circus agents and gain advantage over them by tearing down their posters and replacing them with our own.

Seth was most able at his work, and he had served my grandfather and my great-grandfather before him well over the years. It was through his hard work and diligence that much of my family's success resulted. I think that this very success is what turned him against us, for as our fortunes increased, Seth's remained the same.

It was common for Seth to be away for several days at a time conducting business before reporting to Grandfather, and I decided that I must discover if he was up to mischief while on his travels around the countryside. I would have liked to follow him myself, but I would quickly have been missed and so had to remain in camp. How was I to find out Seth's intent and the reason he was keeping company with a wasp? I wanted to tell Daisy what I had seen, but she didn't see my signals through her closed curtains.

Rufus and I fell to discussing the matter while trying to get to sleep. In the end it was my ladybug friend who came up with a plan.

"We ladybugs all look alike to most people," he said. "And since it's not uncommon to find us roaming free in the countryside, I wouldn't attract attention to myself while in pursuit of our agent. There are lots of ladybugs in our circus, so another could take my place by your side and I'd surely not be missed."

And so we decided that Rufus would follow Seth to keep an ear and eye upon him.

CHAPTER 3

FIRST THING THE NEXT MORNING we went to tell Daisy what I had seen. She was easy to find. Banging an enormous drum, with Queenie, the band bee, humming and drumming alongside, she accompanied the band, who were practicing in full swing.

The blare of brass and scrape of grasshopper were, this early in the day, accompanied by shouts and curses from neighboring caravans. Grandfather, however, was loving it. Standing on the steps of his wagon, dressed in his finest suit, he tapped his cane in time with the music.

Rufus and I joined in. During a break I whispered, "Daisy, I need to talk to you. I wanted to tell you last

night but you closed your curtains. Through my spyglass I saw Seth in the woods, and—"

"Me in my bed!" Daisy said angrily.

"I'm sorry, Daisy. I was just looking to see if you were still awake, because I wanted to tell you what I'd seen."

"You promised your grandfather you'd not go spying on anyone. You'll get wrong with him if he hears of this."

"I wasn't spying, Daisy—it was an accident. Seth just sort of appeared in my view."

"Well, you should have minded your own business and looked away," she said. "And I don't want to know what you saw Seth doing in the woods."

"But Daisy, he was with a wasp!"

"A wasp?" she gasped. "Are you sure? I'm glad I didn't know last night, as it would have given me nightmares! I don't think I want to hear any more about it." But after a thoughtful pause she asked, "What were they doing, Art?"

"I didn't really see much. There was Seth, and another fly, and the wasp. They were talking for a while, and then I saw a glint of light as the wasp passed something to

Seth. I couldn't see what it was. They parted company soon after and Seth returned to camp." I then told her of Rufus's plan to follow Seth.

"You mustn't, Rufus," she scolded the ladybug. "It could be dangerous. You don't know what might happen! You could get lost. And anyway, Art, Seth surely wouldn't do anything to harm the circus, would he? We should just leave it be, or perhaps we should tell your grandfather what you saw."

"No, Daisy. I wouldn't dare. He'd be angry with me even if he believed me, which I doubt. You know how close Seth and Grandfather are. It's up to us to find out what they're scheming, and Rufus's going with them is the only plan we have, unless you can think of another way."

She couldn't. Rufus assured her that he would be fine, and she was finally convinced, though not altogether happy about it.

"I still think we should tell somebody," she said, "but I'll keep quiet about it for just a few days. If we don't find anything out in that time, we either forget about it or let someone know. Now, Rufus, you be *very* careful."

After the band practice Rufus sneaked over to Seth's little beetle-drawn cart, climbed into the back, and hid among the clutter of Seth's belongings.

A short while later they departed and, to Daisy's dislike, I watched them through my spyglass until they passed out of sight down the lane.

CHAPTER 4

AS IS THE CIRCUS WAY, I'D BEEN WORKING and performing since I was just a tyke, and showtime was very busy for me. Before the performance I took the tickets, sold programs, and showed people to their seats, and during the show I did a tumbling act in the first half and walked a tightrope in the second.

As the show was about to start, it was my job to check on the bombardier beetles (who were hidden up around the edge of the great tent) and make sure that they were paying attention. On cue (signaled to me by Daisy on the bandstand), it was also my job to give the order to the bombardiers, and at the drop of my arm they all fired as one and the great tent filled with smoke.

Bombardiers are small, harmless creatures, and their ability to produce a fiery jet of pungent smoke from their bottoms is their only defense against predators in the wild. The noise can be quite alarming, if you're standing too close when one goes off, but the aroma when spread throughout the great tent creates an atmosphere that is particular to insect circuses and is much loved by those in the profession.

Still, it can be a difficult task to get these beetles to act as one, for generally they behave very much like small children. They fidget a lot, have a short attention span, and every time one of them lets off its blast of smoke, he or she breaks into fits of giggling.

That said, we were most fortunate in having a fine fellow named Bill as chief of our bombardiers. He was a great stickler for discipline within his troops, and over the years I had gained his friendship and trust.

But that night, after Rufus's departure, I was distracted and, daydreaming, missed my cue. Unable to contain themselves any longer, the bombardiers, one by one, blew off at the wrong time and started giggling, and that set the children in the crowd off laughing too. From behind the ring curtain, Grandfather gave me a look of great disappointment and irritation.

Clearly flustered by his troops' unchoreographed eruption, Bill said to me, "Sincerest hapologies, young sir. My fellows at arms shall be severely reprimanded. I don't know what comes over them sometimes."

"Bill, you mustn't tell them off," I replied. "It was *my* fault. I wasn't concentrating."

"That's most hunusual, sir," he said. "May I be so bold as to hinquire if something is troubling you? If there is any way we can help, then you only have to hask. You know that we bombardiers can be hentirely trusted to keep a secret: discretion being the better part of valor, as they say."

Not wanting to worry him, I simply said, "Thanks, Bill. It's nothing, really. I'm just feeling a little under the weather."

At last, one hundred glimmering glowworms, which were stationed around the sawdust ring, bathed the arena with their soft light; they also flared up at moments of excitement and could flash in time to the music.

Once the arena was filled with smoke and light, Grandfather, in a splendid pink tailcoat and black top hat, entered the sawdust ring accompanied by a great fanfare from the band.

"My Lords, Ladies, and Gentlemen! Lads and Lassies!" he bellowed. "It's Showtime! Welcome to our Grand Insect Circus, the Greatest Spectacle of this or any age! Be prepared to be amazed! LET THE SHOW BEGIN!"

The great parade entered the ring with all the acts that were to appear. Among a colorful swirl of beetle riders, bugs on bicycles, stilt-walking crane flies, cavorting ladybugs, and such lumbered a massive man, Hercules by name, astride Horatio, the largest stag beetle you can imagine. And right in the center of the action, towering above them all, Sylvia and her snail companions, Sybil and Sally, danced pirouettes on low podiums.

Around the outside of the ring a sparkling green beetle pulled a baby carriage, in which Grimwade the clown sat waving to the crowd and shooting at the children with a water pistol. Scuttling along beside him were the wood lice, Bob and Curly.

After the embarrassment of missing my cue from Daisy I concentrated intently on the matter at hand, and it was just as well that I did.

The last act before the intermission was Little Aunt Emily and her moth, Moonbeam, performing aerial trapeze. Moonbeam was hovering up in the roof of the great tent as Little Aunt Emily climbed the rigging to join her. In the hushed silence that accompanied her dangerous ascent, I noticed movement from behind the bandstand where the rig was tethered and saw the ropes to the trapeze platform go slack. If Little Aunt Emily stood upon it, she would come crashing to the ground!

Frantically, I flashed a signal to Daisy and she dashed to grab the ropes but couldn't reach them in time. Just as Little Aunt Emily stepped on the platform, Queenie, the band bee, flew up and caught hold of the ropes and held them tight.

It was then that I saw somebody running from behind the bandstand. His collar was turned up and

his hat was pulled down to hide his face, and as he rushed for the exit I ran to stop him. He reached the doorway before I did and I chased him outside. Running across the tober, I gained on him and dove to catch him. We crashed to the ground, his bowler hat tumbling across the grass. "You'll not stopped me, you accursed measly scamp!" he shouted as he pushed me off him to make his escape. But not before I had seen his face. Although darkness was descending it was unmistakable: it was Seth!

I stood and watched him run toward the lane and, through my spyglass, saw him climb up onto his waiting cart and make off quickly down the road. I picked up his hat and went back inside.

During the intermission it was my job to sell ice cream to the crowd. Well, I missed it that night for the first time, and the second half of the show found me distracted beyond measure. In the middle of my tightrope act, I lost my footing for a moment and, to a gasp from the audience, I slipped and almost fell.

For the finale I always rode on a saddle high up on Sylvia's back in a procession around the ring. Sylvia and I were very close, and that night she could sense that I was troubled.

"What-th the matter, Art?" she asked me after the show.

I dared not tell her why, for snails are gossipy and they cannot keep secrets.

"I don't know what you mean, Sylvia," I fibbed. "There's nothing the matter with me."

Sylvia knew that I was lying and turning from me said, "Pleathe yourthelf, then. Th-ee if I care."

After the show, Grandfather was waiting to talk to me. He was cross.

"Now that was difficult enough, what with the loose ropes and all, without you causing trouble," he said sternly. "You were wobbling like a jelly on that wire *and* you didn't sell any hokey-pokey during the intermission. It isn't good sense to let the crowd down like that, as they are right partial to their ice cream. You've lost us revenue, my boy. Where did you go rushing off to?"

I was bursting to tell him what had happened but realized that I couldn't without having to tell him *all* that I knew, and how I knew it, and thus getting wrong with him.

"Um. Ah. Well . . ." I stammered.

"Come on, spit it out, boy," said Grandfather, tapping his cane in irritation.

"Well, I think . . . You see, I think I may have had . . ." Blushing to the roots of my hair, I finally uttered, "I had too much birthday cake last night and, well, my stomach—"

"I see," he interrupted. "There's no need to be embarrassed. I suppose that could not be helped, then. But maybe it'll teach you not to go caterpillaring your food down the way you do."

He then noticed the hat that I was still holding.

"Is that not Seth's hat?" he asked me. "How have you come by it?"

"This?" I said. "It was on the grass when I rushed outside. Is it Seth's, do you think?"

"Well, it's a queer thing," he answered, "for it looks very much like his. But I daresay there are others who do wear similar. Besides, I know for a fact that tonight Seth is far from here, scouting a new tober. Now you'd best get yourself to bed, young man, as you've been poorly. And remember, Art, moderation in all things."

Lying on my bed that night, staring up into the sky and wondering where Rufus might be, I was comforted that the moon shining its pale light down upon me would also be his companion. I feared little for his safety, as he had always been a resourceful, courageous fellow, but if I'd known then what I'll now relate I would never have allowed him to go.

CHAPTER 5

RUFUS WAS NERVOUS AND EXCITED WHEN THE beetle-drawn cart left the safety of the circus behind. For hours and hours they rumbled and bumped along until he heard Seth say, "Stopped here, scurvy old beetle," and jump down from the cart.

Rufus cautiously pulled back the canvas covering, under which he'd been hidden, and looked about.

The cart was parked up in the middle of a town, outside an inn named the Wagon and Beetles. It stood beside a great expanse of water. The circus had been here a couple of seasons ago and Rufus knew the place. He was in Diss.

The door to the inn was open, and there was much

coming and going of people and insects. Hoping not to attract attention to himself, he jumped down from the cart, took a deep breath, and followed a farmer and a fly inside.

No one took any notice of him as he weaved his way between the legs of the farmers and merchants that filled the crowded room. He spotted Seth standing at the bar, talking to a stout, ruddy-faced gentleman and settled himself down within earshot of them. He tucked his legs beneath him and pretended to sleep. Seth and the red-faced man talked of nothing but rental for a tober and delivery of sawdust and straw and water and similar mundane matters until Rufus grew very bored and fell into the sleep that he was pretending.

He was awoken by a gentle tapping on his back.

"Come on now, boy. Up you get," said the innkeeper. "Have you been left behind? It's closing time and you can't stop in here. I'll leave you tied up outside. Whoever left you is bound to come back and find you when they sober up."

Rufus was led out of the inn and tethered to a lamppost outside. He waited until the landlord had gone back inside, and with skills that only circus folk acquire he untied himself. Seth and the cart had gone, and Rufus felt deeply embarrassed that he had failed so early in his adventure. The thought occurred to him that they might not have departed long before, and he flew up high into the air in hopes of seeing them. Up above the rooftops and high over the lake he caught sight of them in the distance, on the road heading south. They were a long way off, but Rufus was determined to catch up.

He gained on them slowly and with the last ounce of his strength landed unseen on the cart and quickly hid. In no time at all he was asleep again.

CHAPTER 6

WHEN RUFUS AWOKE IT WAS LATE IN THE night. All was quiet, so he peeked out of the cart to find they were parked up on a village green outside a ramshackle alehouse. Above the door hung a sign, swaying and squeaking in the breeze. Upon it was painted a picture of a hideous insect biting into the neck of another of its kind. Across the front of the pub, in bold red paint, was written PRAYING MANTIS. A shudder of fear made Rufus's wing cases rattle.

Climbing out of the cart, he went to peer in through the alehouse window. The glass was covered in grime, so he rubbed away at it to be able to see in. The first thing he saw in the polished glass was a reflection of Seth's cart beetle staring straight at him.

Rufus turned around and put on his most pleasant face, "Hello there. How are you this evening?"

"Well, that's nice," answered the cart beetle. "Nobody's inquired after my health for many a long year. In fact, I'm *not* very well, as it happens. I've got very sore legs and I'm not as young as I used to be, you know. But who are you and what were you doing in my cart? Are you spying on the master?"

"Oh, no!" Rufus fibbed. "I was just hitching a ride, and I'm a little thirsty, so I was looking through the window to see if I might find a welcome inside. Please let me introduce myself. My name is Rufus."

"Well, Rufus," said the cart beetle, "it's a pleasure to meet you, I'm sure. My name is Noah, and if I were you I wouldn't go in there. The trouble and fighting that go on, well, you wouldn't believe. You stay with me. I have some water here that you are most welcome to, and I would appreciate someone to talk to."

"I'd love to talk, I really would, but I must get into the alehouse. Do you know if there's another way in?"

"You *are* spying on the master, aren't you?" said Noah. "I know you are because I saw you following him earlier today. I don't mind, you know. He's a miserable old sod and I haven't spoken to him for an age. I don't imagine you'll enjoy listening in on him, though—he's very dull. And when he's been drinking, well, a more cantankerous soul you'll find it hard to encounter.

"However," he added, "if you still feel you must go in, there is a little door down the alley that the wood lice use for entrance." He pointed with his foreleg. "Be careful, though, for as I say, they're a rough lot inside."

Rufus peered in through the window at the gloom within. It was crowded, but he could just make out Seth sitting at a table in a dark corner. He was on his own, puffing on a long clay pipe.

Plucking up courage, Rufus ventured to the woodlouse door and poked his head inside. He spotted a low table near the door and quickly scuttled underneath it.

As his eyes grew accustomed to the darkness, he felt a little bolder and casually made his way across the room to within earshot of Seth. Just as he was passing the front door, it crashed open. A fly and a most enormous hooded creature in a long gray cape burst in. Rufus was right in the animal's way, and it gave him a swift kick that sent him head over heels until he came to a stop near Seth's table. Everyone in the bar erupted in laughter but then shortly got back to his own business, leaving Rufus to his. But two mean-looking wood lice up near the bar kept staring at him, so he feigned tiredness and pretended to sleep.

The new arrivals sat down at Seth's table. Glancing up into the hood of the tall figure, Rufus shuddered, for he knew that it could be none other than the wasp that I had seen Seth talking with in the woods.

In a voice as thin as paper, Seth spoke, "Greetings, Jasper, good evening, brother Vince. I trusted that all went well earlier."

"No! I was foiled by a stupid boy," Vince answered, spitting. "The measly wretched gnat tried to stopped my escape, and I losted my nice hat!"

"'Tis a shame, but never minded, brother," said Seth. "We haved the wasp on our side, and nothing will stopped him, eh, Jasper?"

The wasp now spoke, and the way he did made Rufus quake with fear, for he made a curious sound between each sentence like the chewing of rubber bands. "All

arrangements are made *mnk mnk*. Everything goes most well *mnk mnk*. I have the ear of the boss and he sways to my purpose *mnk mnk* and Vince has a key *mnk mnk*. We will be there *mnk mnk*. It will be as I promised."

"How wented the bettings?" Vince asked Seth, rubbing his claws together in anticipation.

"We haved odds of four to one on us winning," Seth replied, "but of course my moneys are on you. All the bets are not yet in, though, so it may all changed. If we played our cards right then we standed to maked a pretty penny by this one, Vince. There is great deals of interest from the flies hereabouts."

"We must taked our leave, brother," said Vince, "as Jasper will soon be missed if we delayed. I must getted him back by first light. We have far to traveled and there is money to collected on the way. You and I will meeted again tomorrow night at the Blue Bug in Bury St. Edmunds. Be there."

With that they rose and left the room. As he strode toward the door past a table of men playing cards, Jasper's cape billowed behind him and flicked a particularly rough-looking fellow across the face. "Hey, pal!"

exclaimed the man, rising to his feet. "Mind yourself or I'll..."

"You'll what?" snapped Jasper, rounding on him, his fearsome head poking from beneath his cowl. "Make a tasty snack *mnk mnk*?"

All of the color drained from the terrified man's face as he slumped back onto his chair. "Ever so s-sorry," he stammered. "It was all m-my fault, I'm sh-sure. M-my s-stupid big face is always getting in the way."

Vince, tugging on the wasp's cape, wheedled, "Not now, Jasper, pleased, not now," and cajoled him out to the street.

Rufus scurried to leave by the wood-louse door and was just in time to jump into the back of Seth's cart as it pulled away.

A little way down the road they turned in to a field and stopped. Unseen, Rufus jumped out and scurried to hide under a bush, from where he kept a watchful eye on his quarry.

Seth built a small fire and put a large pot on it, into which he threw lumps of something from a stained canvas bag. Rufus was hungry and could hardly bear to watch. But when an eddy in the wind brought a whiff of Seth's supper in his direction, the little ladybug instantly lost his appetite. Whatever Seth was cooking smelled quite revolting. Shivering and afraid, Rufus made himself as comfortable as he could in his hideout and settled down for the night.

CHAPTER 7

ON RETURNING TO MY CARAVAN AFTER my talk with Grandfather, my mother had said to me, "Your Rufus seems a little under the weather, Art. I've given him some extra milk. You'd better leave him till he revives."

Rufus's replacement, Rex, was a friendly enough fellow and could be very amusing, but he did not have Rufus's inquiring mind and energy. In fact, what he liked to do most was sleep. And that is how I found him, curled up on my bed.

Daisy's curtains were open and I flashed her a signal. We spent a little while conversing on the matters of the evening. She had not seen the fly in the big top and didn't believe it could have been Seth. She ended by flashing to say that she would talk about it only in the daytime, as she didn't want to have nightmares.

Sleep was impossible, as my mind was in a whirl, and I tried waking Rex to keep me company, but he just snuggled further down into his blankets. I was just able to squeeze through the little window by my bed (as I sometimes did when I was restless) and sat quietly on the caravan's roof and looked up at the stars through my spyglass. But even they did not distract me.

Between our trailer and Little Aunt Emily's was a stout washing line and, when nobody was around, I practiced my rope walking on it. The line shone brightly in the moonlight, and I carefully balanced my way along it.

As I stepped on to my aunt's trailer roof I heard her say, "The snails tell me that there's another big circus in the county. Well, we all know how they like to gossip, but Sylvia was most insistent, claiming that she could smell snails and wasps on the wind."

"No, I don't believe it!" cried my mother. "But do you think it could be them? It couldn't be, could it, for

surely we'd know? Oh, but it would be exciting if it were true. It could only be Uncle William, couldn't it? I'd love to see them all again. But Em! Can you imagine the bundle if we met them on the road?"

"I'd not thought of it, Ell!" Little Aunt Emily replied. "Do you think we should talk to Father?"

"Perhaps we should wait and see if we hear any more," said my mother. "Seth would know if they were within fifty miles of us, and he has not said anything, as far as I'm aware. We don't want to go upsetting Father if it isn't true."

In my concentration, I hadn't noticed that my back was too near to the trailer's chimney pot, and in that moment I became aware of a burning smell—my pajama jacket was on fire! Jumping up to pat out the flame, I lost my footing, slipped from my perch, and just managed to grab ahold of the roof's edge, from which I was left dangling in front of the open window.

"Arthur!" cried my mother in alarm. "What were you doing up there? Have you been listening to us talking?" she shouted. "How *dare* you! If you're not careful I'll give you a thick ear for your trouble! Have you taken to skulking about in the dark, spying on other folk? Is this how your poor Rufus has caught a chill? And have you been smoking? You get yourself down from there this instant and go back to bed! Tomorrow morning I shall find you work to keep you out of mischief. I'll make sure you have no time to go sneaking about. I know—you can tidy up the props wagon. That should knock some sense into you."

I climbed down, returned to our caravan, and tried waking Rex to tell him what I had overheard, but it was useless. He was on his back, sound asleep and snoring, with a most content smile upon his face.

It took me an age to get to sleep, as all sorts of half-forgotten things ran through my mind. Over the years I had heard rumors about Great-Uncle William and the trouble between him and my grandfather, which had led to the breakup of the great Piper circus. And I recalled that the trouble had started over William's desire to get a wasp-taming act for the show. So, here were wasps again. Was this just a coincidence?

CHAPTER 8

WHEN RUFUS AWOKE IT WAS LATE morning and the sun was already high in the sky. Panicked, he looked up and was just in time to see Seth's cart pulling out of the field and onto the road.

Rufus flew after it. It took a while for him to catch up, but finally he landed on the back of the cart and quickly hid again.

Soon after, the cart stopped and Rufus feared that he had been spotted. He lay as still as he could but was still panting from his flight. Seth jumped down from the cart. In the silence that followed, all Rufus could hear was his own heart thumping and then, almost in time with it, a tap tap tapping sound. Carefully, Rufus peeked out. Seth was putting up posters with a little hammer.

Every hundred yards or so, for miles and miles, the cart stopped and started as the fly carried out his business until Rufus heard Seth mutter, "Bother. Pins.

Ranned out of pins. Sharp, sharp pins … Now, I knew I haved more somewhere." Rufus heard him approach the back of the cart. Seth flung back the cover that Rufus was hiding under and found him at once.

"Whoa!" Seth shouted, grabbing the terrified lady-bug and pulling him roughly from the cart. "Who are you?" he hissed. "And what were you looked for in my cart, filthy, sneaking thief, eh? What did you wanted?"

Rufus, engulfed in the foul stench of the fly's breath, stammered, "Please, sir, I was only hitching a ride home."

"Oh, you was were you," Seth hissed. "And where *is* home?"

"Just down the road a little way. In the next village." Rufus answered, spluttering.

"Well you're a lazy, measly grub and should be ashamed for yourself," Seth shouted, throwing Rufus to the ground. "Flyed like any other creature, or toddled on your little legs. Don't expect me to go carted you around. Now buzzed off!"

For the second time in two days, Rufus received a swift kick and went bowling off down the lane.

As the cart passed by him Seth hissed, "If I catched

sight of you again, nasty rotten sneak, I'll maked dishes of your wing cases and feasted off your insides!"

Rufus sat by the roadside, bruised and winded, but, not wanting to lose them again, he rallied quickly and set off after them.

They were easy to follow by the trail of posters. Almost every tree along the lane had one fixed to it with large nails. The posters gave Rufus some comfort, as he realized that if he couldn't carry on then at least he could wait by the road, and that in a few days the circus and I would be sure to catch up.

Wearily, he continued following the posters trail. As darkness fell he arrived in Bury St. Edmunds, where he saw Noah and the cart waiting outside the Blue Bug. Staying as hidden as possible, he worked his way toward Noah.

"Psst, psst, Noah! It's me, Rufus, behind this wall," he whispered.

"Who? Where?" asked the surprised cart beetle, looking all around.

"It's me! Rufus the ladybug! I'm behind the wall!"

"Rufus?" said Noah. "Oh, yes, I remember. Charming fellow. Why are you behind the wall?"

"I'm hiding from Seth," Rufus answered.

"Oh. That *was* you he found in the cart earlier. I thought it probably was, but you ladybugs all look so similar. How may I help you, young fellow?"

"Well, I'm from your circus," said Rufus, hoping that the cart beetle could be trusted. "I'm Art's friend. Do you know Art?"

"I know whom you mean by Art," Noah replied. "That'll be Sir Henry's young grandson Arthur. I've never had the pleasure of speaking to him directly, mind you, but then I've not had the pleasure of speaking to many, as mostly I keep myself to myself. Why didn't you tell me straight away that you are with our circus?"

"I am traveling incognito on very important business," whispered Rufus. "Art and I think Seth is up to no good."

"I could have told you that directly, had you asked me," snorted the old beetle, "and you would have saved yourself a deal of bother in following him. Of course he's up to no good. He doesn't know the meaning of the word." After a thoughtful pause Noah added, "What sort of good is it that you think he should be doing, then?"

"No, you don't understand," sighed Rufus. "Art and I think he may be planning trouble for our circus. Earlier, in that alehouse I heard him plotting something with his brother, Vince, and a wasp. I need to know what it is they're up to."

"A wasp, you say!" cried Noah. "Now, there's a thing. Vile, horrid creatures, wasps. They'll eat your young if you give them half a chance. But I didn't see one earlier. I did see his brother, though, with a tall gentleman, but it wasn't a wasp. Long coat sort of thing. Gray."

"That was the wasp! Inside that coat!" said Rufus.

"A wasp wearing clothes!" gasped Noah. "I've never heard of such a thing. I thought it was only flies that copied that curious human habit. So what was the master doing with this wasp?"

"That's what I'm trying to find out!" Rufus cried.

"Quite right that you should, my lad," the cart beetle

nodded. "If there's anything I can do to help, or anything in my knowledge that you would like to be acquainted with—and let me tell you, I know a thing or two—then you only have to ask." The beetle shook his head from side to side and continued, "I don't like wasps, no sir. I never did and I never shall."

"Well, I should be in the alehouse, watching Seth," Rufus told him.

"Oh, you don't need to hurry," said Noah. "He'll be in there some time, I expect, as he's with his brother, Vince."

"I hope I haven't missed anything," said Rufus as he sneaked nearer to the alehouse's entrance. Unable to reach the door's handle, he had to wait for it to open. A few moments later a farmer stumbled out, belching and burping. Seizing his chance, Rufus ran past him to get inside.

The room was large and full of people and flies, but Rufus couldn't see Seth anywhere and was getting anxious when he noticed some people coming out of a side door. They had left it open, so Rufus went to investigate. The door led to another bar at the back, which was gloomy, and the air was full of tobacco smoke. Seth and Vince were sitting at a table in the corner.

Rufus crept under tables and chairs until he could hear them.

"... orpe Heath, on Monday night," Vince said. "It's all arranged. Jasper, with no small helped from myself I must added, convinced him to come that way. There's great excitement over this one, Seth. We're going to maked a killing."

Rufus was most alarmed by this and furious with himself for having missed their earlier talk. *Who* were they going to kill?

Seth then spoke. "I knowed. All the flies is talking about it. The crowds up there is going to be enormous. I hoped they keeped their head down, though; we doesn't wanted them being spotted."

"Doesn't worry, brother," answered Vince. "We'll be able to retired off this scheme. No more slavings away to filled them Pipers' pockets. We can taked it easy for the rest of our life."

"Yes!" Seth cackled. "It's sorted then. I'll be backed at

the circus two days hence. Comed and finded me. We'll taked out Jasper's share and divided up the spoil."

The flies got up to leave, Seth through the front door and his brother by the back. In a rash moment Rufus followed Vince outside. He watched the fly climb up onto his waiting cart and, taking up a whip, rain lashes and curses down on his poor cart beetle, who set off at a trot. There was nowhere for Rufus to hide in the cart, as it was empty, so he followed as best he could.

On and on in the dark they traveled until Rufus grew too tired and fell behind. The way ahead lay through a wood, and he decided to leave the road, make a nest of leaves under a bush somewhere, and sleep until morning. He was pushing his way into a cozy thicket when a loud voice shouted in his ear. "Ouch! Oi, mate! Mind who you're bumping into why don't you, eh?"

Rufus jumped back in alarm and looked all around, but although he could see the silhouettes of all the branches surrounding him he could see no one there.

CHAPTER 9

COME ON, ART. UP YOU GET NOW," MY MOTHER said, shaking me awake. "You're clearing up the props wagon today. Remember? It's in a terrible mess, and I want you to go through all the costume baskets and sort out what needs mending. Now set to. Up you get. Let's hope it'll teach you to mind your own business."

As little ones, Daisy and I had loved to play in the props wagon, dressing up in its assortment of jumble, but it didn't interest me much now. Everything *was* in a terrible mess—this was going to take me hours or even days to tidy, valuable time that should be spent in investigation! Hours later, all I seemed to have done was to make the mess worse, and I was flagging.

The door opened and Daisy came in.

"I'm here to help, if you like," she said. "Your mother wouldn't let me come any earlier. Were you really spying on her, Art?"

"No, I wasn't! I accidentally overheard her talking with Little Aunt Emily."

"I hope this 'accidental spying' doesn't get to be a habit, Art..."

"I heard Little Aunt Emily say that there is another big circus in the county." I explained. "And mother said that it might be Great-Uncle William's. William's circus has a wasp, Daisy!"

"I wish you'd stop talking about those nasty creatures, Art. I come out in beetle bumps just thinking of them. Anyway, let's get on and get this mess cleared up."

With our combined effort, the work went well and we were sorting out the last of the costume baskets when Daisy exclaimed, "Look what I've found!"

In her hands she was clutching a folder. Stained and tatty, and obviously quite old, it had WILLIAM scrawled in bold letters across the front. We opened it up and tipped out the contents.

First to emerge was a series of scratchy drawings, and diagrams with levers and pulleys and what looked like what might be a beast cage. Then came a fat document written in fading ink. On the front page was written "Notes on the Training of Animals for the Circus by George Piper, circus proprietor: for my sons, Henry and William."

"Let me have a look!" I cried, and fell to reading. Daisy carried on looking through the folder. Suddenly she went very quiet and still; all of the color had drained from her face.

"What is it, Daisy?"

She thrust a folded piece of paper at me and said quietly, "*Our* circus used to have a wasp!"

The poster, for that's what it was, advertised my great-grandparents' circus, and right in the middle of it was a drawing of a turbaned man and a large wasp balancing on a roller.

We pored over the poster. It advertised many wonders, some that I knew and some I had not heard of. My mother was mentioned, beetle riding with her cousin Anne, whom I had never met, and old Grimwade the clown. Hercules and Horatio were also there, but who were the Flying Geminis? Most enthralling of all, in a caption beneath the picture was written, "... from the Mysterious Orient, Mr. Tamari the Wasp Tamer!"

"Wasps again, Daisy!" I shouted.

"It seems we can't get away from them, doesn't it?" she sighed. "But who was Mr. Tamari?"

"I've never heard of him. Let's go and ask my mother."

We showed the poster to mother, and she got flustered and told us to mind our own business and to go and finish tidying. By the time we'd cleared up the props wagon, it was showtime.

Under the distinguished Patronage of the Queen, the Prince Consort, &c.

Mr. & Mrs. GEORGE PIPER'S

INSECT CIRCUS

WILL VISIT THIS TOWN ON

SATURDAY, MAY 6TH, 1882

FEMALE BEETLE RIDERS

Miss Eliza & Miss Anne in Astounding Backward & Forward Feats of Wonder!

BUG JUGGLING !!!
DANCING SNAILS !

THE FLYING GEMINIS

In their Unparalleled Exploits of Tumbling and Equilibria !!!

BICYCLING BEETLES!
BAND & BEE !!!

For the **FIRST TIME IN ENGLAND**, from the **MYSTERIOUS ORIENT**,

MR. TAMARI

☞ THE WASP TAMER !!!

In a Great Cage of Iron, the most daring Exposition of this or of any other age!

HERCULES & HORATIO

England's Strongest Man will wrestle Britain's Largest Beetle !!

The Celebrated English Burlesque Clown

GRIMWADE

Will exhibit his Antics at each performance to Great Roars of Laughter !!

ADMISSION:- DRESS BOXES, 2s. STALLS, 1s. STANDING, 6d. Children under Ten Years of age, Half-price to all parts of the Great Tent. Performance to commence at HALF-PAST SEVEN.

Agent in Advance, Mr. SETH MIDDEN.   Sole Proprietors, G. & E. PIPER.

NO FLEAS PLEASE !

CHAPTER 10

AFTER THE SHOW WE WENT TO FIND OLD Grimwade, the clown. He had been with our family's circus for more than fifty years, and I was sure he would have answers to our questions. The lamp was still alight in his caravan, so I knocked on the door.

"Hello. Who's there?" said Grimwade as he opened the door. "Ah, young Art and Daisy. Do come in, the both of you. I was just brewing up some tea—would you care to join me?"

We climbed the steps and were warmly greeted by Grimwade's two wood lice accomplices, Bob and Curly, who were pleased to have visitors and made space for us on their red velvet sofa. Grimwade sat down at a little table and, peering through tiny spectacles, picked up his sewing.

The caravan was warm and cozy and brightly lit. On a rail up against the wall hung scores of costumes made of silks and satins of every color imaginable.

"Do you like my costumes?" Grimwade asked, looking up from his work. "I have one from every year I've been a-clowning. Some go right back to the time before I was with your great-grandparents, Art, rest their souls. I can't get into lots of them now, mind, but I keep them as reminders of all my seasons on the road. So what can I do for you young friends, or is this just a social visit?"

"Well, Mr. Grimwade, sir," I said, "we found an old poster while clearing out the props wagon and wanted to ask you about the old days."

I pulled the poster out of my pocket and handed it to the gentleman.

"Ah, let me see," said the clown, adjusting his glasses and scratching his head. "Oh, yes, a memorable season, that one! I made a lovely red and blue spotty costume with gold pompoms. Over there, look." He pointed at the clothes rail. "It's too small for me now, and I don't have the hat that went with it, which is a great shame. Some ragamuffin stole it, as I recall. Pretty it was, too. Is that all, or is there anything else you'd care to know?"

"Well yes," I replied, "if it's not too much bother. We showed Mother the poster and she got a bit upset..."

"It's no wonder your mother didn't want to be reminded of the old days," he answered, "for she and her cousin Anne were very close and they haven't set eyes on each other since the troubles, and that's been nigh on fifteen years now. They write when they can, mind, but Eliza still misses Anne so. The breakup of the family hit them the hardest of all."

"Who were the Flying Geminis?" asked Daisy.

"Why, that was Art's grandfather and his twin brother, William," he answered. "As alike as two bugs in a bed, they were, and, although very competitive, were almost inseparable—the very best tumblers in the business. It was a sad day for the profession when they stopped performing together. And a sad day for me as well, I might add, for how I loved to watch them tumbling in their shiny silver suits. They were made

of a quite wonderful material, which the boys would never tell me where they'd found."

"My pops has some silver cloth that he bought for cheering up the band uniforms," said Daisy. "He didn't use it. Shall I ask him if you could have it?"

"If it's the same as that lovely cloth that the Geminis had, then I would be more than grateful," cried Grimwade.

"Who was Mr. Tamari?" I interrupted.

"Yes, Mr. Tamari. Now, his costume didn't amount to a great deal, really. The trousers were a very poor do, just made out of an old pair of curtains, and the top part was nothing to speak of either—bare-chested, he was, with just a skimpy waistcoat! Well, the ladies seemed to like that, but I wasn't so sure it was decent, and all the adulation went to his head and made him a little arrogant." After a short pause the clown added, "He had nice hat, though, of a shimmering butterfly blue, and I was most envious of his pointy-toed shoes..."

"Yes, but who was he?" I asked.

"Why, he was the wasp tamer," said the old clown, looking puzzled. "As you can see from the poster."

"I'm very glad that there are no wasps with the circus now," said Daisy. "I've been terrified of wasps since I was little and can scare myself by just thinking of them."

"You're quite right to fear them, young Daisy," Grimwade said, nodding, "for they are dangerous and unpredictable creatures, and wobetide you if you get stung by one, as I know firsthand. You blow up almost to the size of a snail, and the itching afterward...well, there's not words to describe it! I got a little sting from one once and quickly had to make myself an extra-large costume to wear until the swelling went down. It's that lilac one in the middle there." He pointed again at the rail of clothes. "Of necessity it was a rushed job, and it's *not* one of my favorites. It also takes up a lot of valuable space. Perhaps if I'd put a nice lime green ruffle around the collar and cuffs it may have brightened it up a bit, but never mind—it's too late now to worry."

With this he fell into a silence and looked lost in thought.

"So what happened to Mr. Tamari, and where is he now?" I asked.

"I've no idea where he might be," Grimwade answered, "but he'll be a long ways away from here, you can be sure. Seth and your grandfather see to that."

"Didn't Grandfather Henry like Mr. Tamari and the wasp?" inquired Daisy.

"He liked them well enough," explained Grimwade, "although I suspect he was a little jealous of Tamari's great popularity with the public—especially among the ladies—and he felt sorry for the poor wasp. Now, I don't know how much you've heard about performing wasps, but let me tell you, they are difficult customers and the very devil to tame. It's possible to properly train only ones that are reared in captivity, as the wild kind, having known freedom, can rarely be controlled.

"Well, Mr. Tamari caught his wasp in the woods, and it was as wild as can be. To his great credit he managed to subdue it and get it to do pretty much as it was told, although not without a great deal of moaning and cussing on the wasp's part, I might add."

"Why did Henry feel sorry for the wasp?" asked Daisy.

"Henry is a kindly soul and he loves all the animals in his care," said the old clown. "Now, wasps—there's no two ways about it—are dangerous and unpredictable creatures, as I know firsthand. Oh! I've already told you about that already, haven't I?" he said, taking a wistful look at the large lilac costume. "And for safety's sake they need to be kept contained. Mr. Tamari built a great cage of iron in which to show off his wasp in the ring, and a mighty wagon with bars of the hardest steel to keep the poor creature in at all other times. Henry was strongly against this, as he saw that there was no way that the hapless animal could exercise its legs and wings. He was also a trifle feared of the consequences should it escape into the crowd. Which in time is surely what came to pass."

"Really?" I gasped. "What happened?"

"Well," Grimwade sighed, "it was nearing the end of the season in the year of this here poster, and we were playing to a packed house. It was a good holiday crowd, and they were right noisy and excitable. But for some reason the wasp was in a tricky mood, and as Mr. Tamari was herding it into the great cage of iron, Jasper, (for that was the brute's name) escaped into the tent! As you can imagine, pandemonium ensued. The mighty creature flew round and round, just over the heads of the audience, buzzing and hissing in a most fearsome fashion."

Grimwade paused and drank a large slurp of tea. Daisy said quietly, "I don't think I want to hear any more."

"I do!" I cried.

"A woman, in a very pretty pink dress," the clown continued, "was screaming and waving her hat in the air, and this seemed to enrage the beast and so it flew down toward her and, as she tried to escape, stung her on her bottom!

"Now, Mr. Tamari courageously grabbed ahold of Jasper, calmed him down a bit, and got him back into the cage, but the damage had been done. Before the eyes of the astonished crowd the poor woman began to swell up. Henry rushed to his caravan and brought back some vinegar, which, when applied to the sting, helps a bit with the swelling, and to her credit, the woman did not want to leave. Those sitting either side of her shuffled aside a bit to give her space, and the show went on. By the time of the finale, she was taking up three seats, and after the performance she had to be carried out in a wheelbarrow, for she could barely walk."

Daisy was looking very pale, and Grimwade said, "There's no need to worry yourself, my dear. The lady survived *and* she came back to see a later show, free of charge."

"It wasn't her I was worried for—it was me!" said Daisy. "Do you remember the season that Pops took me to Jim Carner's Coleopteran Cavalcade to learn beetle riding tricks? Well, sometime toward the end of the tour, I was resting in our trailer eating an apple when I heard a fearsome buzzing. Suddenly, an angry wasp came scrambling in through the window and grabbed the apple from my hand! Quick as lightning, Pops pushed the vile beast back out with a broom and slammed the window shut. I hid under my bed and dared not come out for the rest of the day!"

"You've never told me that before," I said.

"I've never been more frightened in my life, and I try to put it out of my mind," she said.

"Well, I think you're lucky, Daisy. I've never seen one close up."

"You wouldn't want to, Art, you really wouldn't."

"I bet I would! Anyway, what happened after the wasp attack, Mr. Grimwade?" I asked.

"Enough was enough for Henry, and he said the wasp had to go. That led to a great argument between Henry and his twin, William, which ended with them agreeing that they could no longer work together and that the circus must be rent in two.

"At the end of the season they divided up all the tents and carts and animals and such in a fair fashion. The girls obviously went with their fathers, Eliza and Little Emily with Henry and Anne with William. All of us performers had to choose which brother to go with. This we decided on the toss of a coin: heads with Henry, tails with William. As you can see, I spun heads.

"The very next morning," the clown continued, "the two circuses left the tober through the gate onto the lane. William and all those with him turned left up the road and Henry and all with him turned right."

"And Mr. Tamari and Jasper went with William?" I said to Grimwade.

"Of course they did, my lad!" he chortled. "How could they not have?"

"Have Grandfather and William seen each other since?" I asked.

"Not a chance," said Grimwade, shaking his head. "It was agreed between the brothers that William would keep to the western counties and Henry to the eastern, and that's the way it's been ever since the split."

"Besides," he added, "it's just as well we've never bumped into them upon our travels, for you can imagine the bundle that might ensue if we did."

I certainly could, for in circus lore there are countless tales of the fierce rivalry between circuses for good tobers and crowds. I imagined that it would be most exciting to take part in such a fight, but as our circus was the largest in the eastern counties we were never threatened. Any circus bundles that I had heard talk of were confined to the smaller troupes. Their main aim was to put the opposition out of business for the remainder of the season.

It was getting late and since I didn't want to get into more trouble I thanked Grimwade for all that he had told us and we got up to leave.

"It brings back fond memories, talking about the old days," he said, his familiar grin now fully restored to his face. "Now before you go, let me ask you two something: I've heard people say that red and green should never be seen, but I think they look lovely together. What do you think? Perhaps if I add a little gold braiding? Or is that too Christmassy?"

"That would look fine," I said. But Daisy disagreed. "The red and green would look much better if you add a touch of turquoise instead of gold."

"Thank you for that, young lady." Grimwade smiled. "I shall do as you suggest."

As we were leaving Grimwade looked up from his sewing, "You'd do well to keep that poster tucked away, as it may upset folk, and especially you're not to mention Mr. Tamari to your grandfather Henry, as he may fly into a rage."

Now, I don't want to give the impression that my grandfather had a bad temper, for that was very wide of the truth. He was a gentleman in the true sense of the word, and was most loving and affectionate to me and all of the family, as well as with the animals in his care. But I took notice of the clown's advice and tucked the poster firmly into my pocket.

Daisy and I were left full of wonder from our conversation with Grimwade. I'd always known that Grandfather had a brother, William, but I never knew that they were twins!

I walked with Daisy to her caravan and then went home to bed. Rex was there, sleeping peacefully, but I had less luck getting to sleep. I tried flashing a message to Daisy but she'd closed her curtains again. In that moment I missed Rufus badly. I wanted to tell him all that we had found out, and I was curious to know what he may have discovered. To pass the time, I read my great-grandfather's notes on animal training, but it only made me more wakeful, for in the section dealing with wasp taming I read, "Wasps are undeniably *the* most dangerous animals shown in the circus ring. I cannot stress the importance (if either of you should choose the path of tamer, and I dearly hope that you don't) of keeping a respectful working relationship with a wasp, but at *no* time can they be trusted!"

CHAPTER II

WHILE I LAY AWAKE FRETTING, MANY miles away Rufus confronted the stranger in the dark wood. "Who's there? Where are you?" he demanded.

"Calm yourself, mate. I'm Woody." A leafy branch came down toward Rufus and gave him a little shove. "Standing right here in front of you, little chum."

Rufus jumped backwards. "Whoa!" he cried. "A talking bush! What are you?"

"I'm no bush, mate," said the voice, laughing. "Look."

Rufus backed away, still afraid, as many leafy branches shook in the moonlight.

"Can't you see me?" asked the voice. "Look!" The

shaking began again, a lot slower this time. "Oh, never mind, mate. Just you take my word for it. You'll be able to see me in the morning."

Rufus wasn't sure he wanted to stay until morning—he felt like running off there and then, but the mysterious voice continued, "Lots of people can't see me straight off, especially in the countryside. I can understand why, I suppose, but it upsets me sometimes. I'll let *you* off though, mate, because it's dark."

"What are you?" Rufus asked again.

"I'm a stick insect. You've never heard of one, have you, my little friend? It's not too surprising, as there aren't that many in this country, and most of them are with the circus."

"Which circus?" Rufus asked, forgetting his fear for a moment.

"Different ones around the country. Mostly in the south, where the weather's warmer. I've been with one myself. Anyway, that's enough about me. What about you, mate? Who are you and what are you doing here tonight? Are you on walkabout?"

Not wanting to reveal his true purpose, Rufus said,

"Oh, I was left behind at the inn by my master, and I'm taking a shortcut through here, trying to catch up. My name is Rufus."

"Well, like I told you, my name's Woody," said the stick insect, "and I'm glad to meet you."

Through the darkness a small branch came toward Rufus. He gently shook it.

After a silence Woody said, "I suppose you'd better get going, then, if you're chasing your master."

"Oh, there's no great hurry. So which circus were you with?"

"They were called Seeth and Bidwell's Great Ant Show," Woody answered, "and I was their major sideshow attraction. It wasn't around here but a long way off, down on the north coast of Cornwall, where the surf reminds me of home."

"Where is your home?"

"Australia, mate," said Woody. "I came over here by accident. I got myself into a spot of bother in Sydney Harbor and was hiding up in the rigging of a ship when the blessed thing set sail. Many weeks later we docked in Plymouth. Been here ever since. I've grown to love it here over the years. It's a mite cold in winter, but the tucker is real good, and when I find what I'm a-looking for I'll be as happy as a greenfly in a rose garden.

"Anyway, small fry, I was telling you about the ant show," he continued. "I got work with them soon after arriving. Bit of a novelty I was, and I enjoyed the ants' company until all their endless committee meetings started getting me down. The people were worse, though. It gets very tedious having them looking at you all day long and poking you to make you move. 'Look Mummy, it's a walking stick,' and 'Oh, leaf him alone,' and if I hear that 'What is long and thin and brown and sticky?' joke one more time, well, I don't know what I'll do."

"What *is* long and thin and brown and sticky?" Rufus asked, confused.

"Why, a stick, of course," sighed Woody.

"So what are you doing so far from Cornwall?" asked Rufus.

"I am looking for a mate, mate. I've heard a rumor that there's a lady Woody traveling with a circus in these parts, and I'm trying to find her."

"Well, I've not heard of her, and I've been with a circus around these parts all my life." Rufus said and then quickly blushed to the color of his wing cases, for he straightaway knew the mistake he had made. What a fool he felt, and what a useless spy he was! He couldn't pretend for five minutes without revealing his true identity.

"So you're with a circus, are you, little one?" asked Woody excitedly. "You don't say. It's near hereabouts, is it? Quick! Let's go after your master together. Come on! Which circus is it?"

"Piper's Circus," answered Rufus truthfully, now that he had blown his cover.

"Why, what strange fortune—that's the very one! That's the name I was told! Where are they? Quick, let's go and find her."

"The circus is nowhere near, and I am sorry to tell you that there is no lady Woody with it," said Rufus. "And I wasn't following my master home. I was trailing someone else, and I've lost them. I just came into the woods to sleep."

"Well, it's crook to hear that about the lady Woody, Rufus. I had it on good authority that she was with Piper's. Who is it you're following, then, my mini mucker?"

Rufus told him.

"I saw a geezer on a cart like that not long ago, going down the lane," said Woody. "We'll find him in the morning—no worries. Feel free to stay the night here.

I'm plum tuckered out myself from all this talk and disappointment, and I'm to sleep. I'll see you in the morning, mate."

"And I hope that I can see you, too," answered Rufus as he snuggled down into a pile of leaves.

CHAPTER 12

I WENT TO SEE DAISY EARLY THE NEXT MORNING. Her father, Chester, was cooking breakfast on an open fire beside their caravan. Chester Cheyne was always humming or singing. "Good morning Arthur-rarthur-omp-pomp-pomp. How are you this fine day-hey?" he asked.

"Very well, thank you, Mr. Cheyne," I said. "Is Daisy up yet?"

"She's jolly-wolly not the lazy bo-wo-wones," he sung. "Stand-aland beneath her window-ow and serenade-ade-ade her awake. You sing-aling the words while I hum-pum-pum the tu-une in accompani-pumpani-ment."

Thankfully, Daisy poked her head out of the caravan door and I was saved from embarrassment.

"Would you two tra-la-love bugs care to join with me in some bar-bar-breakfast and a sing-aling-along?" asked Chester.

"Thanks, Pops, that would be lovely, but we can't. We said we'd go and see the snails this morning. Sally's babies are due to hatch today, and we don't want to miss that, do we, Art?"

"Don't we?" I asked. "Oh, no, of course not! Come on, we'd best be off, then."

"Sorry about that," Daisy said, grimacing, as we left Chester to his breakfast, "but he *does* mean well."

CHAPTER 13

AFTER A VERY GOOD NIGHT'S SLEEP, RUFUS AWOKE in the woods.

"Good morning, Rufus," Woody greeted him. "You're a wee sleepy head, aren't you? You'd best get up right quick if you're to catch up with whom you're following. His trail will have gone cold by now."

Rufus focused on the bush in front of him. Woody really did look like a stick with six leafy twigs—most definitely an insect, though. He had a wide grin on his face.

"Only joking." Woody laughed. "As they say, 'The early spider catches the fly.' Well, I've been out and caught one, too. Your chum is camped up in a field beyond the wood, fast asleep in his cart. If you get down there now you'll catch up."

"Thanks for your help," said Rufus. "I hope you find your lady Woody, Woody."

"Now, you're real sure she's not with the Piper circus, my pocket-size pal?" Woody asked.

"She's definitely not."

"Oh, well. I guess I'll head back west and ask around," Woody sighed. "It is very odd, though, for I was told it was certain." But the smile quickly returned to his face when he said, "Never mind, eh, little cobber. I know she's around somewhere." Getting up to leave, he continued, "Come on. I'll show you where the fly is and then I'll be on my way. Now, why did you say you were following this geezer?"

As they made their way through the wood Rufus told Woody about all that he had seen and heard on his travels, about the wasp and the flies and the killing that was to happen at Orpe Heath.

"Well, wee fella, that *is* a scary tale! I reckon I'd better stick around with you to make sure you're safe, if that's all right with you?"

"Oh, yes!" exclaimed Rufus. He was relieved at the thought of Woody's company, for in truth he had been a little nervous on his own.

Nearing the edge of the wood, Rufus became worried that he'd be seen. Woody didn't have to be as cautious, blending perfectly with his surroundings. The cart was pulled up in the shade of a tree, with Vince still asleep in it. His cart beetle was grazing nearby in the early-morning sunshine.

Rufus edged as near as he could and hid under a bush to keep watch. Not long afterward, Vince awoke and was exceedingly grumpy. "Hurried up, you wretched beast," he shouted at his cart beetle. "Tethered yourself to the cart and getted me home as fast as you can. I haved much to do today."

The beetle hurried to strap himself into the carriage as Vince pulled his cooking irons out of the fire and kicked about in the rubbish that was strewn around it. They left shortly after.

Rufus followed them along the road, with Woody keeping to the hedgerow alongside. After hours of trudging they came to the outskirts of a town and took a rest beside a large sign that read WELCOME TO NEWMARKET, THE HOME OF BEETLE RACING. Beneath, roughly painted on a board, were the words, "The police constabularyment of this localitry do commandeer all visitators to keep their ladybugs on a leash. (Penaltry for disobeyance £1)."

Woody was worried. "I'm a rare sight in these parts, and I'll stick out like a sore claw if I go through town, mate. I don't wish to alarm anyone. I'll work my way round through the gardens and try to keep you within sight. And you be careful, little friend."

Rufus chased after Vince's cart. It had stopped by the clock tower, waiting for a team of race beetles to cross the road. They had large numbers painted on their wing cases and gaily dressed riders upon their backs.

The whole town was full of bustle and noise. All along the busy main street beetles, carts, and carriages clattered up and down or were tethered outside the shops, hotels, and alehouses. All sorts of grand people were promenading, dressed in their finery, and there were flies everywhere.

Rufus followed the cart up the street. The sidewalk was so busy that to keep Vince in sight he had to keep to the side of the road where he was in great danger from the passing vehicles.

Unnoticed by Rufus, a small beetle cart, driven by a rakishly clad young fly, was cutting through the traffic, traveling at speed toward him. Too late, Rufus jumped aside to avoid the oncoming vehicle, and its wheel clipped his back and sent him spinning into the middle of the road, where a large brewery cart, loaded with barrels, bore down upon him.

Just in the nick of time a rather portly police constable appeared, wobbling along on a bicycle, and nimbly scooped Rufus into his arms.

"Ho ho! Well, what curiositry do we have here?" he asked jovially. "An enscaped animal that is unattached from its master, if I am not greatly misplaced." In a loud voice he exclaimed to the crowd, "Can I have your attentionment, please! I have an announciation! Have any of the assemblary here presence misaquired a ladybug?"

All heads turned to look but nobody came forward to claim Rufus. The smiling policeman said to him, "Well, my little vagabondage, you shall just have to accompanance me to the police stationary, where I am duly bound to compound you until your disobeyant owner is found and the one-pound penaltry is paid."

Having no notion of what being compounded entailed, and not liking the sound of it at all, Rufus grew alarmed and in a bid to be free bit the policeman hard on the thumb.

"You scoundrelry!" squealed the constable as he dropped the little beetle to the ground.

Rufus scuttled away as the policeman made a lunge

to recapture him. The terrified beetle just managed to evade his grasp by unfurling his wings and taking to the air with what strength he could muster.

The policeman remounted his bicycle and, holding his throbbing thumb aloft, chased after Rufus, shouting, "Stop this instance, you botherous villaination!"

Rufus flew up and over the heads of the crowd and glanced behind him to see his pursuer gaining on him fast. With the policeman alternately shouting for him to stop and blowing his whistle, they raced up the busy street.

To Rufus's great fortune the road began to steepen a bit as it headed out of the town and, after several perilously close swipes from the pudgy constable's hand, inch by inch the terrified ladybug widened the gap between himself and his adversary.

He was tiring fast and could fly no more. Having gained a little distance, Rufus landed in the road and as fast as he could manage scurried into a garden to find a hiding place. In an instant he was grabbed and pulled into a bush, where he was enveloped in a rustling of leafy limbs and hidden from sight. It was Woody.

"Hush," whispered the stick insect. "Stay still."

They waited in silence by the roadside as the purple-faced policeman approached, peeping on his whistle and puffing from his exertions. As he passed by, Rufus heard him mutter, "I'll recapturate you, you mischievance, if it takes me all day!"

Rufus stayed nestled in Woody's green embrace and watched the police officer pedal on up and over the crest of the hill, where he disappeared from sight.

"Get yourself in a spot of bother, did you, mate?" asked Woody.

"Oh, Woody!" Rufus caught his breath. "I'm so glad to see you. That was awful! I was going to be compounded!"

"Ooch, mate!" The stick insect took a sharp intake of breath. "That sounds painful."

"Yes, and to make matters worse, I've lost Vince. I am as good as useless at this spying business, Woody."

"You're not as bad as you think you are, my little friend, for you found me, didn't you? And I know where Vince is! He went by here not five minutes ago and drove through that gateway up the road there."

"Is he still there?" asked the ladybug.

"I expect so, although I haven't yet looked, for I got distracted. See, I found a privet hedge!" Woody said, and held out a dark green leafed branch. "Try a bit, chum. It's good."

Rufus took a bite and then spat it out, disgusted at the bitterness.

"Hey, mate, don't waste it! It's one of my rare treats, and for some reason or other it only seems to grow near towns."

When Woody had eaten his fill and Rufus had recovered a bit from his ordeal they walked up the road and peered through the gateway into the field where Vince's cart had gone.

All of the color drained from Rufus's face. "How can this be?" he exclaimed. Filling the field, and looking just like he'd left it those many miles behind, was the Piper circus!

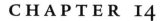

CHAPTER 14

THE BABY SNAILS HADN'T HATCHED YET, and Daisy and I found Sylvia, Sybil, and Sally deciding on what to call the impending arrivals. Daisy got very excited and came up with all sorts of suitable names. I offered up Cedric and Cecil as possibilities. But Sylvia was clearly still annoyed with me from the other night and scoffed, "Don't be thilly, Art. You know our naimth always thtart with an 'eth.'" I left Daisy with the snails and went home to have something to eat.

As I was crossing the tober, I saw Seth's cart pull into the field and park outside Grandfather's caravan. The fly climbed down and went in to see Grandfather.

So Rufus was home! I kept watch on the back of the cart, expecting Rufus to appear, but he didn't. Growing concerned, I went to investigate. There was the usual rubbish in the cart, which I began to pull about, but there was no sign of Rufus. Suddenly I was grabbed from behind. Seth had quietly come out of Grandfather's caravan and caught me!

"Oi! You scurvy whippersnapper!" he shouted at me. "Getted yourself right out of my cart this moment! What are you doinged, eh?" He pushed me out of the way and began to rummage about in his belongings, making the muddle even worse. He was muttering to himself, "Sneaking, mangy thieves. Twice in one week! Twice! It's not right, and where wented my pins?" Turning to me he hissed, "Had *you* gotted my pins?"

"No, sir, I'm sorry sir," I said. "I know nothing about your pins. I was only looking for some old posters that I could use to draw on."

"You asked me first, boy," he said angrily. "My cart is my business and you keeped your nose well out of it. I will watched you from now on, you scurrilous scallawag. I doesn't liked the looks of you. And you shan't haved no old posters. They're mine. All mine. Now buzzed off before I beated you black and blue."

I spent the rest of the day in extreme agitation. Where was Rufus? I was so worried that I couldn't eat my lunch, and my mother, thinking I was ill, sent me to rest on my bed until showtime.

CHAPTER 15

ON SEEING THE CIRCUS CAMPED ON THE NEWMARKET tober, Woody shouted, "Rufus, you're home!"

"I don't know," said Rufus, troubled. "There's something strange about it. It doesn't feel quite right, and how did it get here?"

"No idea, mate, but it looks great to me. I'm going to ask around and find out if anybody knows about the lady Woody. I've got a strong feeling that I'm getting close. Come on. Let's go in."

Woody boldly started off across the grass toward the circus, and Rufus had no choice but to follow him.

As they neared the wagons and caravans parked all around the great tent, Rufus called out, "Woody! Stop!"

Woody froze like a statue. "What is it, little fella?"

"It's that beast wagon over there," said Rufus. "There's a wasp in it!"

"Where?"

"Over there," said Rufus. "Next to the wagon with the..."

"Lady Woody in it!" the stick insect hollered, and set off at a run.

Rufus scurried after him, trying to keep up.

Inside the wagon the lady stick insect looked stern. As Woody arrived she gave him an irritated look and asked, "Where *have* you been? I'd given you up for lost, mate. You were supposed to be here in the spring."

"I'm sorry, petal," said Woody as his green face reddened. "I'd no idea where you might be until a month or so ago, and it's taken all this time to get here." Sticking a limb through the wagons bars he stammered, "H-hi. I'm right pleased to meet you at last. My name's Woodrow, but everyone calls me Woody."

"I'm Honeysuckle," she said with a smile. "And *you* can call me Honey. Come on in—the door is open."

Rufus left them to get to know each other and

crept off under the wagons to explore. He was confused and a little frightened, for all around him was familiar and yet very different. As he passed under the wasp cage, the occupant sensed his presence and started hissing and snapping its jaws. "I can smell *mnk mnk* a sweet suppery smell *mnk mnk,*" it snickered. Rufus hurried past.

It was then that he caught sight of my grandfather coming out of his caravan door. Rufus rushed forward to greet him but soon stopped dead in his tracks. There was something strange about Grandfather: he had a long mustache! Grandfather had never had a mustache.

Rufus backed away to regain his hiding place, but he had already been seen.

"Hey, you!" shouted "Grandfather" at him. "You should be practicing with the others in the great tent. Get in there at once!"

Warily, Rufus made his way toward the tent's entrance and poked his head inside. In the ring, ladybug acrobats were clambering up on each other's backs to form a living pyramid. Rufus ventured over to them.

"Who are you and what do you want?" said a rather gruff voice from the bottom of the pile. "You'd better be quick—we haven't got all day."

"I want to know what circus this is and if I may be able to join you," Rufus said, thinking quickly. "I have long wanted to be in the circus and have fun all the time like you do."

Groans of "Oh, no, not again!" and "This gets *so* boring" came from the balancing ladybugs.

The topmost fellow called down, "Look, son, we get a lot of you local lads wanting to run away with the circus. It's not all fun and frolics, you know. It's hard work, and you have to be skillful and fit. So what is it that you can offer us? Can you tumble?"

"Why, yes, I've been practicing for weeks."

"Show us what you can do, then," said the ladybug.

Not wanting them to know of his circus skills for fear of being invited to join the troupe, Rufus turned a couple of head-over-heels, fell over onto his side, and, rolling onto his back, waggled his little legs in the air. The kindly ladybug, not joining in with the others' laughter, said, "Get on your way, son. Go back to your mother. But, keep practicing. You never know—one day you may be fit enough."

"Excuse me, though," pleaded Rufus, "you never told me the name of this circus."

"Can't you *see* the wagons outside and what is painted on them all?"

"Sorry, sir, I've seen them, but I cannot read," Rufus lied.

"Well, I'm very sorry to hear that," the ladybug said gently. "It says 'Piper's Circus.' Now good day, son."

"Please, sir, which Piper circus?"

"Oh, for goodness' sake, will you please just go away?" shouted the gruff ladybug. "There is only *one* Piper circus, you fool: Sir William Piper's circus."

Well, Rufus was no fool, for he knew more than this ladybug did. There wasn't only one Piper circus, there were two, and he was currently in the wrong one.

CHAPTER 16

WOODY AND HONEY WERE CUDDLED up together in the corner of the cage, looking just like a pile of leaves. Rufus coughed loudly. "Sorry to interrupt, but I've got to get back to Art right now, and I've come to say goodbye."

"What are you talking about, little fella?" asked Woody, yawning. "Isn't *this* your home? You said you were with Piper's Circus."

"I am," answered Rufus. "But it's not this one. There are two!"

"What? Two circuses with the same name? That's a bit crook, isn't it? Are you sure?"

"Yes, I'm certain. But there isn't time to explain. I must get back to Art as quickly as possible."

"Tell me about it on the way," said Woody, standing up. "I'm coming, too. It's the least I can do for you after having led me to my Honey here. I could even fly with you some of the way, if you like."

"I didn't know that you could fly."

"Course I can, mate." Woody laughed. "But I don't do it often, as it seems to alarm people when I fly past. We can leave as soon as you like."

"You'd better not be gone long, sweetheart," Honey sighed. "I've spent enough time waiting for you already."

"Don't fret, pet," he said. "I'll just see my tiny pal home and then come straight back. I promise."

Rufus and Woody set off, back towards Bury St. Edmunds, on the long journey home. All that night and all the next day, they flew a little and walked a lot.

CHAPTER 17

FROM MY BED, LATE IN THE EVENING, I finally caught sight of Rufus slowly plodding up the lane. As he reached the gate I watched him turn around and wave back down the road.

Mother opened the door for Rufus with a quizzical look. "What are you doing up?" she asked him. "I didn't see you go out. You look dreadful. Get back into bed at once and I'll bring you some warm milk."

Fearing that my mother might see him, I pushed Rex into the corner of the bed and covered him with a blanket. He was sound asleep and didn't stir.

Rufus was clearly exhausted.

"I'm so glad you're home," I said, hugging him.

He replied feebly, "Oh, Art. You won't believe what

I saw…in the county…there's another Pi…" Before Rufus could complete the sentence, he fell into a deep sleep from which I couldn't wake him. I desperately wanted to know what had happened to him, but it would have to wait.

The next morning, when the coast was clear, I woke Rex and told him it was time to leave. He was most reluctant to go, since he'd had the best week he could remember, but with a deal of grumbling on his part I ushered him out the door and went to find Daisy, as she, too, would be eager to hear Rufus's tale. When we got back to the caravan Rufus was awake and fully revived.

"Oh, Rufus!" said Daisy. "I'm relieved you're back safe! I've been so worried for you. Has it been hard?"

"You won't believe the time I've had," Rufus gushed. "I've been halfway around the county, and made a new friend or two."

"Was that who you were waving to down the lane?" I asked.

"One of them, yes. That was my trusty companion Woody."

"Tell it from the start," pleaded Daisy, and Rufus

related his great adventure. What excitement he had had! I then told him what we'd been up to and had discovered, and we tried to make some sense of it all.

It clearly hadn't been Seth cutting the platform ropes a few nights before, so it must have been Vince. "Why would he have done that?" we wondered.

What we *did* know was that Grandfather had a twin brother whose great circus, the very match of our own, was in the county and had a wasp in the company. Something bad was going to happen on Monday at someplace called Orpe Heath, at which Seth and his brother Vince were going to kill someone in front of crowds of hiding flies and make a great deal of money, if they played their cards right.

So there was clearly gambling involved, but neither Daisy nor I could think of any card game that would make a good spectator sport and that would involve murder. Very worried, we decided to talk to Grimwade again, to see if he could help. One of us also had to keep watch on Seth, for sometime that day he was due to meet with Vince, and I was determined to be there when he did.

CHAPTER 18

AISY AND I SET OFF TO FIND GRIMWADE, and Rufus went to resume his watch on Seth. On the way out we passed my mother.

"You're looking more like your old self, Rufus," she said to the ladybug. "I am glad to see you have revived. Now, make sure that Art doesn't tire you out today."

Grimwade was not in his caravan, and Daisy and I eventually found him playing skittles in the great tent with Bob and Curly. We sat and watched them for a while. Bob set up six skittles in a triangle. Curly then curled himself into a ball (which is the wood-louse way) and Grimwade picked him up and rolled him force-fully at the skittles.

Although Grimwade's aim was not very good, all the skittles were knocked over, for the wood louse stuck his little legs out and steered straight to the middle of them. As the skittles came tumbling down, Grimwade, Bob, and Curly shouted, "Hooray!"

After a few more turns, Grimwade noticed us watching and came over to talk.

"Good morning, Art. Good morning, Daisy," he said cheerily. "Daisy, thank you for your advice yesterday. The turquoise works extremely well with the red and green, and I think the whole ensemble will be very fetching. Now would you both care to join me in a game of skittles? I'm afraid you'd not have much chance of beating me, for I am a consummate player and, as you no doubt will have observed, my aim is remarkable. But you are welcome to try me if you wish."

"Thank you, Mr. Grimwade, we'd love to," I said. "Can we ask you some questions as we play?"

"Of course you can, my boy. Fire away, both with your questions and with the ball."

Not wanting to hurt the wood louse, I rolled it very gently toward the skittles. The little animal veered off to the right and crashed into the ringside. He looked up at me and said "Ouch."

"Stand aside there, young man," said Grimwade. "I'll show you how to do it." He rolled a terrible shot, but still all the skittles fell down. "Technique, my boy, technique," he assured me.

Daisy picked up Bob carefully. She, too, seemed hesitant at the thought of throwing the little fellow, and she gave him a nudge toward the skittles. It looked obvious to me that he was going to stop well short, but slowly, picking up speed, he went hurtling toward the skittles and they all came tumbling down.

"Hooray!" shouted the wood lice. "Well done, Daisy!" cheered Grimwade. "You're a natural!"

I had better luck as the game went on, and Daisy's score was high, but as we all knew, Grimwade was sure to win. All the while that we played I asked him questions.

"Have you heard of Orpe Heath?"

"No, Art—whoops, mind there, oh, and another lot goes crashing down—I don't believe I have," said the old clown.

"Well, do you know of any card games in which somebody gets killed?"

"Gets killed, eh?" Grimwade looked troubled. "I've not heard of anything like that and wouldn't care to. You'd best keep away from games like that, Art. Practice your skittles, instead—you clearly haven't taken in all the advice from my marvelous little *Sharpen Your Skittling Skills* book."

I was getting nowhere.

"Do you know where William's circus is now?" Daisy asked him.

"They're out there somewhere entertaining the public I daresay, but I have no idea where," he told her. "A long way off, though, I'm sure. Seth's brother, Vince, is William's agent, and he and Seth are under strict instructions to make sure the two circuses are always counties apart. Ooh! Did you *see* that lovely shot of mine?" Curly had rolled a complete turn around the ring before sending the skittles flying in all directions. "Anyway, the last I heard tell they were somewhere along the Welsh border, but that was in the spring, back when the lovely yellow daffodils were out."

I wanted to tell him that we knew otherwise, but how could we explain how we knew about Uncle William's circus without Rufus and I getting into trouble?

Grimwade won the skittles match with one hundred points to Daisy's ninety-five. I scored fifty-one with which I was quite happy considering the little practice I had had. After we thanked Grimwade, Bob, and Curly for the game, I set off to find Rufus, and Daisy went to see if the baby snails had arrived yet.

CHAPTER 19

RUFUS WAS HIDING UNDER A WAGON from where he had a good view of Seth's cart. I crawled under to join him. The cart was there but neither Seth nor his cart beetle could be seen.

"Has anything happened?" I asked.

"Seth's in the caravan with your grandfather. He came out a little while ago to get something from the cart."

We lay in silence for quite some time, and I had just thought to go and find Hercules and Horatio to ask them if they might have heard of Orpe Heath when a dark shadow loomed over us and a voiced boomed, "There you are! I've been looking for you all over the place. I am glad to see that you've arrived home safely."

"Shhh!" hissed Rufus. "We're hiding!"

"That's not as clever a place as behind the wall," said the voice. "I can see you. Is it a game? Do I get a prize for finding you?"

"No! It's not a game. We're watching Seth!" Rufus whispered.

I rolled out from under the wagon and stood up to introduce myself.

"Hello. You must be Noah. I'm pleased to meet you and sorry I've never spoken with you before. My name is Art."

"And it's my great pleasure to meet you, too, young sir," said Noah. "I know your name well and you have no need to apologize for not talking with me, for mostly I am ignored and have grown accustomed to it. I trust it is due only to the company I keep," he said, nodding in Seth's direction, "and nothing to do with my character." Noah then stuck his head under the wagon. "Are you going to come out from under there now, Rufus?"

Rufus bustled out from his hiding place, looking a little cross.

"I've been hiding there for ages," he snapped at the cart beetle, "and you've given the game away. What if Seth comes out again? He'd be sure to see us, and then where would we be?"

"So it *is* a game, then?" said Noah. "But I don't know where you'd be, apart from where you are now, I suppose, unless you move first, of course. Oh, dear! You must explain the rules to me. This game seems very complicated. Why are you watching Seth today? Is he up to no good in the caravan with Sir Henry?"

"We're keeping an eye on him to see what he does next," I told Noah. "He's due to meet his brother, Vince, sometime today, and we want to be there to over-hear what they say. We don't know when it will be, so we're keeping watch."

"Oh," said Noah, still a little perplexed. "Why didn't you just ask me? I could have told you and saved you the bother." Lifting up a front leg, he pointed down the hill, "Ten o'clock tonight, after the show. Down that lane there a little way in the wood, by the ford. Shall I see you there?"

"No, Noah!" I said. "If you do see us, you must

pretend that you *haven't*, for we must not be seen. We could get into all sorts of trouble."

"Right." Noah nodded. "I think I've got it now. A clever but tricky game. If I see you, I haven't seen you. Yes, I think I could do that. Right." Turning to Rufus, he inquired, "And how was your journey home? I was a little worried about you after you disappeared into the Blue Bug."

CHAPTER 20

I THANKED NOAH FOR THE INFORMATION, arranged to meet Rufus later, and went off to see Hercules and Horatio. They were sitting out in the sun in front of the long wagon that they shared as home.

The strongman, Hercules, and his stag beetle partner, Horatio, had been with our family circus since my great-grandparents first started it way back when. Every night in the ring, they wrestled in a staged fight that always left Hercules the victor. It was a grand sight as the sawdust flew up and the earth shook as one or the other of them crashed to the ground. They were both enormous. The strongman had a rugged face that looked as if it were hewn from granite, and he was still immensely powerful despite his now quite advanced years. Hercules was his performing name. His real name was Timothy. He was a very gentle man, extremely shy, and he had not spoken more than a dozen words to me in all my life. Horatio was not the stag beetle's real name, either. His name was Horace.

Seeing me approach, Horace called out, "Hello, sweetie! Have you come to join us? How nice! Look, Timothy, Arthur's come to join us. Isn't that pleasant?" Timothy blushed deeply, nodded, and smiled.

"Would you like some gâteau?" Horace asked me.

I devoured a large slice of the delicious cake and we passed the time of day. I kept trying to steer the conversation around to talk about the old days, and Great-Uncle William, and all that was on my mind, but Horace's concerns were more immediate.

"You don't want to go worrying about all that, dearie," he said to me. "That's done and dusted and all tucked away nicely in the past where it belongs. Now, have you *seen* the baby snails? Hatched not an hour ago, they did. They're darling and they're tiny enough that even you could pick one up, Art, and there are such a lot of them. You must go down and say hello. Take some flowers for their mother, Sally. She would love that."

It was relaxing to sit in the sun for a while and talk with Horace and Timothy. Their good nature and their great size were comforting, and being with them I felt that nothing could possibly go wrong in the world.

Showtime was approaching, though, and as I got up to leave I asked if either of them had heard of Orpe Heath. "Orpe Heath? No, I don't think so, petal," Horace replied. But Timothy was trying to say something. His face was getting redder and redder until finally he managed to squeeze out the words "No" and "Sorry" in a very small voice.

CHAPTER 21

As WE WERE PREPARING FOR THE PERFORMANCE, I told Daisy about Seth and Vince's ten o'clock meeting. Rufus and I had agreed that after the finale we would make our way to the wood by the ford and hide in a good spot to overhear them. The show was usually over by a quarter to ten, so if we were quick we would have just enough time to get there first. I asked Daisy if she would come with us.

"I can't, I promised Pops I'd help him polish the brass instruments and pack them for the move tomorrow. If you go without me, though, I'll worry, for it could be dangerous. Isn't it time we told your grandfather about this, or perhaps we could just ask Seth what's going on?"

"You know we can't tell Grandfather, Daisy. He'll think we've been spying and get cross," I insisted. "And I wouldn't *dare* ask Seth. Would you?"

Daisy shook her head.

"It's settled, then," I said. "We're going."

"Well, if you're not back by eleven o'clock," said Daisy, "then I am going to raise the alarm."

By seven-thirty the audience was seated and I was waiting to give the bombardier beetles their cue, but Grandfather did not appear. I became a bit anxious that the show would run late but didn't want to get too nervous in case I wobbled on the tightrope and irritated Grandfather.

Bill sensed my agitation. "You seem a trifle troubled hagain, young sir. I hope you're not still feeling hunder the weather? Now, we don't want a repeat of the other hevening's performance, if it can be havoided."

"I'm fine," I replied. "I just don't want the show to run late."

"Got an hassignation, have you, sir?" he asked, giving me nudge.

"A what?"

"An hassignation," he repeated. "A meeting with an hadmirer?"

"No, it's nothing like that. I've just got to be somewhere at ten o'clock."

"You're not in hany bother, are you, master Art?" he fussed. "If you are, I trust you know that you can halways rely on us bombardiers to come to your haid and hassistance?"

Before I could reply, the time came for the bombardiers to fire, and they all blew off at once. I was most attentive to my jobs throughout the performance, wanting neither to draw attention to myself nor to be responsible for any more delay, as we were now running alarmingly late.

Eventually, the finale came and went, and after quickly feeding Sylvia (who was still in a sulk with me) I ran out as fast as I could to meet Rufus. We had to rush all the way to the ford, and we were both panting hard by the time it came into view. We were late, for Seth's cart was drawn up right in the middle of the river, from which Noah was drinking.

"Get a moved on, you idle slug," Seth hissed, cracking

his whip over the poor beetle's back. Noah moved on slowly and they drew up on the other side of the ford beside a giant willow. Gripping a shovel, Seth climbed down from the cart and disappeared behind the tree.

Rufus and I headed upstream a little, crossed the river, and cautiously made our way toward him to see what Seth was doing. He was digging a hole, down between the roots of the tree.

Pushing a claw into the earth, he pulled out a cloth-wrapped parcel and, snickering to himself, carefully unwrapped a shiny metal box. This must be what I had seen Jasper giving to him the other night! Seth opened the box and pulled out a fat wad of banknotes. He sat on the ground and began counting them into two large piles and one smaller one. I could hear him muttering: "One are mine and one are Vince's. One are mine, one are Vince's and one are for Jasper. One are mine and one are Vin—"

Suddenly, I was grabbed by my collar and thrown to the ground as Rufus sailed into the air in front of me, having received a violent kick. "What mischievous miscreants haved we here?" Vince hissed. "Spied on my

brother, would you? Measly sneaks. Oi! Seth! Looked what I've catched! Little bits of supper, unless I'm much mistaken."

I'd never before seen Seth fly, but he did then. In an instant he was upon us, flapping his wings madly and wielding his spade above his head.

CHAPTER 22

AFTER THE SHOW DAISY GATHERED UP WHAT instruments she could carry and joined her father by their campfire.

They sat in silence for a while, cleaning the trombones and trumpets until they sparkled in the firelight. Daisy worked especially hard, trying to take her worried mind off the trouble that Rufus and I might be getting into.

"You're a trifle-ifle quiet, my pop-pop-poppet," sang Chester. "We usual-usually sing-aling as we pop-pop-polish. Is there something that trouble-bubbles you this tra-la-lovely evening?"

"I'm sorry, Pops, but I'm a little concerned about the

baby snails. They get ever so restless, and I promised Sally that I would look after them for a while so that she can get a little rest. The poor thing has to work very hard tomorrow with the move."

"Run aling-along there now if you want to. I can finish the polly-olly-olishing on my lonesome-ownsome."

Feeling guilty for lying, Daisy set off, past the snail stable, to the tent in which Sorrel, her ring beetle, was tethered. As she ran, she heard her father call out behind her. "Ba-ba-be-bop back within the hour or I'll start to wirry-worry!"

CHAPTER 23

SETH LOOMED OVER ME. "YOU AGAIN! IT'S THE filthy, mischievous thief I catched in my cart!" he screeched at Vince. Looking at Rufus, he screamed, "And I knowed you—you're that other spiteful sneak, the one who stealed my pins! Shall I killed them, Vince? Shall I bashed them with my spade? Robbed my money, would you, you pathetic, loathsome slugs?"

"Let's eated the boy and buried the ladybug in that hole, Seth. The boy looked tasty. Who is it, Seth? Does we knowed who it is?"

"I knowed who it is all right. It's Arthur, the old worm's darling grandson, and he wanted our money but he's not going to get it 'cause we're going to killed him and we're going to eated him!" With a hideous gurgling he lifted the spade high above him and brought it flying down toward my head. I thought my days were numbered, but at the last possible instant Vince knocked the spade aside.

"No! Stopped!" he shouted. "I've just thinked of something. We can't killed him now—it'll ruined our plan and be our undoing, for your miserable circus would not be moved tomorrow night if this scurrilous rogue is missing. We're going to have to letted him go for now. We can killed him and eated him on Tuesday when the deed is done."

Seth was not pleased to be missing a good meal and set about cuffing me in a flurry of scratching claws. Vince pushed him aside. "Calmed yourself, Seth, and savored the pleasure of waiting for the feast!"

Seth snatched me and Rufus from the ground and dragged us to the road, where Noah was waiting with the cart.

Holding us up in the air for Noah to see, Seth said, "Look! We've catched the nasty, mangy rascals that was rifled in the back of our cart!"

Noah looked up from nibbling the grass by the roadside. "Nasty, mangy rascals? Where?" he said, winking at me. "I can't see anyone, I can't see a boy and a ladybug."

"Stupid, stupid beetle," spat Seth as he dragged me and Rufus down the road to the ford and threw us in the river.

I spluttered to my feet and looked around for Rufus. He was floating downstream, and as I ran to grab him I slipped and fell back into the water. By the time I had picked myself up, he had turned a bend in the river and was out of sight.

I set off after him, afraid that he would drown. The water ran fast and deep at that point, and I had to pick my way carefully along the bank. Struggling around the turn in the river, to my great joy and surprise, I saw him. The river had widened and there he was, right in the middle of it, cradled in Daisy's arms.

"Daisy! How did you get here?"

"I was so worried after you left that I had to follow," she said. "Sorrel carried me as fast as she could down the lane. When we heard shouting, we jumped the hedge and headed straight across the meadow to the river. As we got to the water's edge I saw Rufus racing toward us upon his back, and I waded in and scooped him up as he was going by!"

We dragged ourselves out of the water and Rufus appeared to be none the worse from his ordeal. Daisy and I, however, were a sorry sight. Our clothes were soaked and filthy and I was badly scratched from Seth's frenzied attack.

We made our way slowly back up river to the ford. Seth and Vince were gone.

CHAPTER 24

WHAT HAS HAPPENED TO YOU BOTH?" my mother cried as we entered the caravan. "Art, your face is all cut, and Daisy, just look at the state of your clothes! What will your father say? What *have* you two been doing?"

Utterly exhausted from our doomed adventure, I began to tell her the truth: "We were down by the river watching Seth and he..."

"Have you been spying again?" she snapped. "Well, you probably deserved all that you got, then. You're behaving very oddly of late, young man. Get out of those wet clothes right now. It's bedtime for you. I don't know what I'm going to do with you, I really don't."

"But he was going to ki—"

"THAT'S ENOUGH NOW!" she shouted. "It's about time you learned to respect your elders. You leave poor Seth alone! He doesn't want to be bothered with you; he already has enough on his plate."

"Not as much as he nearly had," I mumbled to myself.

Mother turned to Daisy and said softly, "Come on, my dear, let's get you into something dry. I'm very sorry if my boy's been leading you into mischief."

"It's not like that," said Daisy, "Seth really was about to—"

"Daisy," Mother interrupted, "I'm surprised at you. Don't tell me that you've been spying too?"

"No. But—"

"That's enough!" said mother sternly. "Come on. Let's get you home."

Rufus and I slumped into bed and I soon fell into a fitful sleep. All night long I dreamt of Seth and the spade and the racing river, and in the early light of morning, unable to stand it any longer, I quietly got up. I woke Rufus and we crept outside. Noah and the cart were again pulled up outside Grandfather's caravan. Seth was snoring in the back of it.

Today was Sunday, moving day, and I knew it would be a long one. Still no nearer to finding out what dreadful deed was to occur on the morrow and having no idea what to do about it, we went to call on Daisy.

No one was up, so I threw pebbles at Daisy's window to wake her. She looked up, quite startled, and opened the window. "You gave me such a fright. What do you want so early?" she whispered.

"We're going to see the baby snails," I called up. "Do you want to come with us?"

"Shhh! Keep your voice down, I'm in trouble enough with Pops, after last night. Just be quiet and I'll be out in a second."

Several long minutes later she appeared and we set off. On the way I picked a bunch of buttercups, which I presented to the snails' mother, Sally. She was very pleased and polished them off in an instant.

Daisy played with the baby snails and I tried talking with Sylvia, who was ignoring me.

"Good morning," I greeted her.

"Ith it? Well, it ith a day off for you, I thuppothe," she replied, "but uth thnailth have lot-th of work to do taking down the tent-th, and we've the long pull to the necktht tober to look forward to thith evening. It'th all right for you, you can just thleep all the way there."

"I'm sorry that you're upset with me, Sylvia. I haven't meant to be difficult with you, but I've been a little troubled these last few days and I didn't want to burden you with it."

"What trouble, Art?" (She was warming to me a little.) "Pleathe tell me all about it."

As it seemed like there was nothing that I could do to prevent the events of the following day, I thought it would do no harm to tell her and let the gossip begin. I told her everything.

"Art, what a thcary time you've had! That nathty fly Theth came here earlier to th-ee the new arrivalth. He wath drooling and muttering thumthing about lovely with garlic. He giv-th me the creepth, Art, he alwayth hath." Turning to her friends she called, "Thally! Thybil! Come and lithen to thith. Go on, Art, tell them all that you jutht told me."

And so I repeated my story to Sally and Sybil and the baby snails.

"We knew that there were other thnailth in the county—we could thmell them on the wind," Sally said.

"And wathpth, too," added Sybil. "We've been telling folk but they haven't believed uth. What do you think the fly-th could be planning, Thylvia?"

"It thounds to me like creepy Theth and his thtinky brother Vinth might be thetting uth up for a bundle ath a gambling opportunity for their fly friendth! Evil little fiendth. We must be on our guard, girl-th, and we must make plan-th."

"What do you mean?" I asked. "Setting us up for a gambling opportunity and a bundle?"

"Why, Art, can't you th-ee it?" Sylvia asked. "The've organithed the whole thing. Thumtime in the night, ath thure as thnailth eggth are thnailth eggth, we will meet William'th thircuth on the road. Theth and Vinth are taking bet-th on the outcome of the fight. Oh my word, what can we do? We mutht find out the where-about-th of Orpe Heath and be on our guard."

"A bundle," gasped Daisy. "No!"

"Why do you think that Vince undid the rigging the other night?" I asked the snails.

"To demoralithe us, I thuppoth," said Sally. "If Little Aunt Emily had plummeted to her death, we'd all be in a thorry th-tate now, wouldn't we? I ecthpect Theth and Vinth have bet a lot of money on William'th thircuth winning the fight."

"Shouldn't we tell Grandfather about the bundle?" I asked her. "We could change our route and avoid it."

"He wouldn't believe uth, Art," Sylvia sighed. "It may be thtupid, but he would trutht Theth with hith life. They have worked together for such a long, long time. Apart from the animalth, there'th no one who would believe uth, I'm afraid. All we *can* do ith be alert."

"Well, the least we can do is spread the word so that all can be on guard," I said.

Sylvia went to tell the show beetles in the stable tents, Daisy left to tell Queenie and the grasshoppers, and Rufus and I set off to see the bombardiers.

I found Bombardier Bill and told him of the impending fight.

"You can count on us, Master Art, sir. If we are needed," he said, standing to attention, "just give us the horder. We'll make sure we're primed and ready with our smelliest smoke, and we'll all be serious and not giggle—halthough that may be hard for some of the younger ones."

Warning of the forthcoming bundle spread around the camp like wildfire and by midmorning a great chattering of insect voices could be heard on the breeze.

At lunchtime my mother said to me, "There's a deal of commotion coming from the animals today. Do you think there is a storm brewing?"

"There very likely is," I replied, not wishing to incite her to anger again by telling her the truth. Besides, I was feeling better now that the animals knew what was to come.

The rest of the day was spent packing for the move. In the early evening the great tent was taken down, folded up, and put on a wagon with its poles. To avoid congestion on the roads, we always traveled at night, as we could only move as fast as the slowest of us, the snails. They could manage a speed of about four miles an hour and were able to travel a distance of twenty miles or so before becoming too tired to carry on. Tonight they were set for a long haul, eighteen miles to the next tober near Bury St. Edmunds.

I sat up on the seat of the caravan with my mother as Sylvia pulled us along. Rufus climbed onto the roof for a better view of any trouble on the road ahead.

At about midnight, my mother told us to go to

bed. I tried pleading with her to let us stay awake, but without any luck. As soon as I was settled in my bed I took out my spyglass and resumed my vigilant watch. Due to my restless sleep of the night before, the gentle rocking of the caravan, and the warmth and comfort of my blankets, in no time at all I fell fast asleep.

CHAPTER 25

I AWOKE FROM MY SLEEP WITH A START AND crashed to the caravan floor. Rufus and an assortment of bedding and pillows rained down upon me. From outside came a great hullabaloo—shouted curses and a loud jangle of insect voices. I nervously pushed open the door and by the light of the full moon an extraordinary sight met my eyes. We were at a crossroads, and blocking the way ahead was a circus quite the image of our own.

All around the caravan there was a kerfuffle of men and insects, raging and fighting like a stormy sea. Up in the air, beetles, moths, and crane flies were bumping and crashing into each other in chaos.

From high up in the sky, an enormous dragonfly swooped down and dropped large rocks, narrowly missing Rufus and me. We jumped to the ground and, just as we had scuttled under the caravan to safety, a mighty boulder smashed the step of the wagon to splinters.

Crawling out, we dashed to Daisy's wagon, but she wasn't there. Right beside it, Chester and his band were assembling and setting up their music stands. Shortly after they started playing I became aware of different music coming from another band nearby. Chester obviously heard it too, for he shouted to his players, "La-la-louder my tra-la-la-lads! La-la-louder! We'll showdle-owdle them who's the ba-ba-ba-ba-best!"

The rival band also got louder and louder, and soon the air was filled with a cacophony of battling brass and scratching grasshopper.

I was searching for Daisy when I saw Sylvia in a tussle with another snail. Back and forth they pushed each other, first one having the advantage and then the other. I felt for Sylvia, for I knew she must be exhausted after the long hours on the road. She saw me watching and, while pushing with all her might, gasped, "You mutht find the wathp wagon, Art! The beatht must not be allowed to get free! Do what you can! It'th over there." She gave the other snail a great push in the direction I was to go.

I told Rufus to find the bombardiers and bring them to me at the wasp cage.

As I wove my way through the melee, I noticed my mother wielding a great frying pan in her hand: she was shouting at a woman who carried a large bowl of eggs. Then I came upon Grimwade.

He was carrying a water pistol and a bucket, engaged in a shootout with another clown who was similarly equipped. They stalked each other around a cart (under which four wood lice cowered), firing their weapons.

Grimwade popped his head up over the cart and, grimacing, took careful aim but missed his opponent entirely, and some other poor fellow caught it right in the face. Now this made both the clowns laugh, and so they carried on, firing at each other and missing and chortling at other's misfortune. Everyone around them was getting wet and dirty, but Grimwade and the other clown stayed dry and clean.

A tremendous cloud of dust signaled the arrival of Hercules and Horatio. And their foes. Hercules was with another giant, and they were looking around keenly. "That'll do," said the unfamiliar strongman, pointing at the back of a cart. Resting their elbows on the back-board the two huge men locked hands to arm wrestle. As they shook from the exertion of their equally matched strength, their faces grew redder and redder.

With jaws entwined Horatio and the other stag beetle were crashing about in the dust. Horatio's adversary was quite a bit smaller and was clearly losing the fight. Suddenly, with a loud crack, one of the poor creature's jaws snapped off.

"Oh!" gasped Horatio. "I'm most terribly sorry, dearie!"

"Don't worry, poppit," replied his rival. "It was only glued on anyway. Look, this one comes off too." The beetle then bashed its other jaw on the ground and off it popped.

"But, how...?" Horatio said, and then laughed. "Oh, I get it, sweetie! You're a female in disguise!"

Ducking and diving my way through the bundle, I

caught sight of the mighty wasp wagon, its steel bars glinting in the moonlight. My heart missed a beat as I saw that Vince was unlocking the massive barred door. The wasp inside was in an extreme state of agitation, buzzing fiercely and looking desperate to get out and join the fight.

I ran at Vince, crashed into him, and bowled him over as we went tumbling across the grass. I was desperate to keep him away from the cage until rescue arrived, but he was far stronger than I. He also had the advantage of more limbs with which to hit me, and a much longer reach. I was soon overpowered. As he pinned me to the ground I noticed over his shoulder that Jasper, the wasp, was trying to turn the key that was still in the cage's lock. It appeared to be all over—we would soon be defeated.

Vince's hideous face looked down at me and I was enveloped by his foul-smelling breath. "So, you're in a hurried to be eated, are you, you vile, mischievous boy?" he snickered. "Can't you waited for tomorrow?" He placed his hideous claws around my neck and started to squeeze. As I tried to roll away I felt the spyglass in my pocket and struggled to grab it. I freed it from the tangle of my clothing and with what strength I could muster swung my arm out and up in hopes that the weight of the telescope in my hand would knock his claws from my throat.

But Vince had tightened his grip and I was losing consciousness. Time seemed to be slowing down. As if from a distance, I saw my arm swing in an arc. I watched as the spyglass slowly extended until, as it reached its full length, it cracked Vince such a blow to the temple that he collapsed on top of me.

As I wriggled from underneath his smelly weight, Jasper finally managed to open the lock to his cage. I staggered up amid the angry buzzing of the wasp and tried to push the door shut. It was useless, for all my strength had gone.

A voice called out, "Need a little help, mate?" I couldn't see who it was at first, but as a bushy branch rushed by I realized it must be Rufus's friend Woody. He pushed hard against the door and locked himself across it like a wooden brace to jam it shut. But the strength of the mighty wasp was too great for Woody,

and he soon started bending and shaking. He looked as though he might crack like a dry twig as the door inched open.

In the nick of time, Bill and the bombardiers arrived!

"Quickly!" I shouted to Bill and his company. "Shoot at the door! Shoot at the door!" Bill roared, "Hattention!"—all the little bombardiers lined up, pointing their bottoms in the air—"Ready!—Haim!—Fire!" And they let off as one into the opening cage door. Jasper reeled back, repelled by the smoke and the stench as Rufus and I rushed in to slam the door shut. I turned the key, removed it from the lock, and put it in my pocket.

Woody had collapsed on the ground, and Rufus rushed to him. "Woody, are you all right?" he called. The dazed stick insect slowly raised his head. "Yeah, little fella. I think so. Nothing's broken, mate, but what was that dreadful smell?"

CHAPTER 26

N THE CALM THAT FOLLOWED, I BECAME
aware of two angry voices shouting loud enough
to rend the sky in two. Right in the center of the
bundle, Grandfather, red-faced and fuming, was waving his stick and shouting at his living double! The
only apparent difference between them was Great-Uncle
William's long mustache.

"You ancient buffoon, you!" shouted Grandfather.
"Get your ill-begotten contraptions, and your rabble,
out of my path!"

"Your path, you old has-been?" William snorted.
"*Your* path? Your miserable array of contrivances and
sickly creatures are insulting the queen's highway!
Remove them from the road!"

To and fro they traded insults and shook their sticks. The bundling all around them began to subside as heads turned to watch and listen.

"You trespasser, sir, you are a disgrace!" cried Grandfather.

"Well, sir, you are a bounder! You are a bully!" William parried, poking his stick.

"You are a ne'er-do-well. You are a blackguard!" exclaimed Grandfather, stamping the ground.

"You, you, you villain!" William countered.

"You vagabond!" came Grandfather's reply.

"You scoundrel!"

"You ruffian!"

"You rogue!"

"Josser!"

"Slug cuddler!"

"Earwig!"

"Fleabag!"

With this there was a moment of angry silence and then, in unison, the two roared, "I WILL NOT TOLER-ATE . . . THIS OUTRAGEOUS . . . BEHAVIOR . . . FOR

ONE MOMENT LONGER!" With sticks flying, they set upon each other in a most desperate fashion.

There came a sickening crash as they collided and fought with stick on stick. They looked as if they were performing a most curious country dance as in turn they thwacked each other on the back or the legs.

Their crazy duet went on and on until with a mighty crack to the shin Grandfather felled William. As he hit the dirt William grabbed ahold of Grandfather's tail-coat and pulled him down to join him. In a wild jumble of flailing limbs and sticks they rolled around in the road, still cussing.

It's strange, but at no time during their fight was the spectacle anything other than mesmerizing, and the longer they fought, the more I began to enjoy it (for which I felt a trifle guilty). Somehow, it was beautiful to watch. As I pondered this, I noticed a change in the language that was coming from the swirling mass. In place of the oaths and curses came a "Whoa up!" and an "Over!" and a "Hup!" and then in unison a "NOW!" and they split apart and went tumbling around in the road! Back toward each other they came and with a great spring and bounce one was up on the shoulders of the other and then back down again. They did forward flips and backflips, and turned cartwheels and somersaults in the best display of acrobatics that I have ever seen. Two old gentlemen, with more grace and agility than you may see in men half their age, tumbling for joy!

As the light of an early dawn appeared, the assembled crowd watched with mouths agape. After several more minutes of astounding tumbling, Grandfather and William bounced to a full stop, took a quick breath, and then locked hands to take a deep bow in front of the amazed audience. At that very moment, the sun made its arrival and lit up the old gentlemen in majestic splendor. Applause, whistles, and cheers erupted from the crowd as Grandfather and Great-Uncle William carried on bowing for a full five minutes.

The praise from us all was loud and strong, but it didn't quite hide the sound of hissing and booing that was coming from the trees and bushes all around. Everybody stopped to listen.

In that moment Daisy screamed "No!" and scooping up a rock from the ground threw it at Grandfather and Great-Uncle William as if her life depended on it. With mouths agape, the crowd watched the projectile as it sped toward its target.

CHAPTER 27

WIELDING A LONG HIDEOUS BLADE, Seth charged at my grandfather. As he plunged the knife toward Grandfather's heart, Daisy's perfectly aimed rock struck the dagger and sent it flying through the air until it clattered to the road by my feet.

Seth flew to regain the knife as I put my foot down hard upon it. "I'll not forgetted you, you worthless, detestable skulk, and I'll getted you when I can! You see if I doesn't!" he spat.

In a flash, the evil look upon his face was replaced with a simpering smile. He turned, fell to the ground, and groveled at my grandfather's feet. "Please, please don't punished me. I promised I will never tried to harm you again, good and kind master." This was answered by a terrific uproar of booing from the surrounding bushes, but Grandfather was speechless at the betrayal of his trusted servant. Sylvia filled the silence. She briefly told Grandfather of the events of the last week and of Seth and Vince's wicked plan.

Looking all about him, William asked, "Has anybody seen Vince? Has he been here this night?"

I spoke up and told them all that had happened by the wasp wagon, and I blushed as I told Grandfather how I had used the spyglass as a weapon. Somebody went to fetch Vince. He had barely revived from the blow I had given him, and he joined Seth, wretched, at the old gentlemen's feet.

"Why did you want to kill me, Seth?" my grandfather asked him plainly. Seth hung his head and did not answer.

"If he had killed you, William'th thircuth would have appeared to win the bundle," explained Sylvia, "and they could have kept their profit-th from the bet-th. Ath it ith, with the fighting over and nobody the winner, they will have to pay everything back, and more, I darethay. They thall be ruined."

"So let that be their punishment," said William. "Let us give them to the flies."

"And what of Jasper, brother?" asked Grandfather. "He has had a claw in this."

"He must go," he replied reluctantly. "He came from the wild. Perhaps I should return him to it."

Grandfather and William escorted Seth and Vince up the road to where their carts could now be seen in the morning light. "Go now and never let us see you again," said Grandfather.

Seth and Vince climbed up into their carts and picked up their whips and the reins.

"Moved on, Noah. Getted you going," Seth said, trying to exude an air of confidence. "*Nk Nk*. Walked on! *Nk Nk!* Getted your flea-bitten carcass on up the blasted road, you loathsome slug!" But Noah would not move. Vince was having the same trouble with his cart beetle.

I looked around for Daisy, but she'd disappeared again, so Rufus and I went to speak to Noah. We thanked him for all his help and said goodbye.

"Hello, young Art. Hello, friend Rufus," he said cheerfully. "It's a great pleasure to see you this fine morning, but why are you saying goodbye? Are you going away?"

"It's not us that's going away, Noah," I explained. "Seth *was* up to no good and has been banished. I supposed that you would be taking him away."

"Seth?" inquired Noah. "I don't believe I know anyone by that name, Art. I think I might have used to, but my friend Norah here and I have a clever new game. It's called We-don't-know-anyone-called-Seth-and-Vince-and-even-if-we-did-then-we-wouldn't-be-able-to-see-them-anyway. It's a good game, Art. I could teach you the rules."

"I'd like that very much." I winked.

Seth and Vince finally realized that they were on their own and, climbing down from their carts, nervously started walking up the road. They had nothing with them but Seth's money box. As crowds of angry flies moved in toward them from the bushes and trees, we left them to their fate, turned around, and went back to the important business of the day. We had a show to put on that afternoon.

I walked back with Noah and he said to me, "It's a grand day for the insect circus, Art. This bundle will be remembered for generations to come. What do you think they might name it?"

"I imagine it will be called 'The Bundle at Orpe Heath,'" I answered.

"Why Orpe Heath, Art?" he asked with a puzzled look on his face. "This place is called Blackthorpe Heath."

"Did you know we were coming here tonight, Noah?" I asked him.

"Why, of course I did, Art. I always know where we're going next."

"Well, why didn't you tell us?"

"You never asked," said Noah.

CHAPTER 28

ACK BY THE CARAVANS AND WAGONS, TABLES had been laid out with cups and plates and toast and jam, and a wonderful smell of frying bread filled the air. Mother was with a woman that I knew straightaway must be her cousin Anne. They, along with Little Aunt Emily and a bustle of women—some known to me and others not—were talking and laughing.

Daisy was talking with Sylvia. We were all so pleased to see each other safe and sound. "Thank you for saving Grandfather!" I said. "That was a terrific shot with that rock."

"I must have improved my aim after playing skittles with Grimwade," Daisy answered modestly.

Jammed together around a small table, Horace and the female stag beetle were head to head in a quiet conversation, and Timothy and his new strongman friend were comparing the size of their muscles. To my delight, the usually speechless Timothy was talking happily.

Woody and Honeysuckle were nowhere to be seen and I imagined that they were off somewhere, happy in each other's company.

Grimwade and his rival clown were sitting at a table with a massive plate of food between them. Laughing hysterically, they pulled silly faces and flicked baked beans at each other. Daisy and I joined them.

"Welcome, young heroes of the fight," said Grimwade. "What a splendid way to start the day! A brilliant bundle, the finest performance by the Flying Geminis I've ever witnessed, *and* a big breakfast! What fun, what joy! I must thank you both for your inestimable parts in this morning's fine entertainment, and may I have the honor of introducing you to my friend Bagshaw."

It was a pleasure to make the clown's acquaintance, but one thing still troubled me. Where was Mr. Tamari?

I had been nervous of his appearance since the start of the bundle and still half anticipated his arrival. I asked Grimwade and Bagshaw if they knew where he was. They pointed their forks in the direction of Grandfather and Great-Uncle William, who were sitting together, deep in conversation.

"Over there," said Bagshaw. "Talking with your Grandfather."

"Great-Uncle William is Mr. Tamari?" I gasped.

"Of course he is," said Grimwade, flicking a bean at me. "Everybody knows that, don't they?"

Timidly, I approached Grandfather, anticipating a punishment for the misuse of my spyglass.

"Young man," he said to me, "from what I can gather, it seems that you've been using your birthday gift for everything but the purpose for which it was intended. Perhaps I should confiscate it until you're a bit older and wiser. What do *you* say, brother?"

"It's clear to me that this strong-willed lad has disobeyed you, Henry. But"—William winked at me— "it must be said that, in this instance, the end most definitely justified the means." And, slapping me on the back, he added, "Let the good fellow keep it!"

"All right, then, I shall," said Grandfather. "But be careful where you point it, Art," he warned. "And remember, 'Curiosity killed the caterpillar.'"

I promised them that my spying days were over and that I would confine my telescope's use to studying the starry sky.

After we'd all eaten our fill, and sprains and bruises had been tended to, we pulled the wagons, carts, and caravans into a huge circle on the heath and put up one of the great tents in the middle. Word of the morning's events had spread through the neighborhood, and that afternoon hundreds of people gathered for the show. Somehow we managed to fit them all in to the great tent, and I stood with Rufus and Bombardier Bill, awaiting my cue from Daisy.

It was the grandest day of my life, and my proudest moment was when I dropped my arm for the bombardier smoke to blow off as Grandfather and Great-Uncle William together proclaimed, "My Lords, Ladies, and Gentlemen! Lads and Lassies! Welcome one and all to Sir Henry *and* Sir William Piper's Grand Traveling Insect Circus! The Very Greatest Spectacle of this or *Any* Age! Be Prepared to be Amazed! LET THE SHOW BEGIN!"

Notes on the
Training of Animals
for the
Circus

By George Piper, circus proprietor:

for my sons,
Henry & William

My dear boys,

You have now reached the age when it would be wise
to decide upon which kind of creatures you would
care to present in the great circus ring. To aid you
in your choice, I'm jotting down these notes on
the training of animals, learned from my long years
in circus life.

I'll begin by relating that it is not possible to
teach a creature to do anything that it would not do
by habit in its everyday life. This is <u>most</u> important
and should never be forgotten. It's just not right
to make a creature behave in a way that is not within
its nature.

In yesteryear, when there was scant understanding

between beast and man, animals were made to perform by harsh and sometimes cruel methods. To our great good fortune this is no longer the case. In recent times (and I am proud to say I have been a party to this), it has become the practice to treat all animals with kindness and understanding. Known as the 'gentling' method, this way can achieve surprisingly successful results, along with rewarding one's charges with their favored comestibles.

Of the countless variety of insects, mollusks, and such like, in the known world, only a very small selection have found their way into circus life, and listed below are the more usual performing creatures, along with some that are less common. The majority of animals are cooperative, if handled properly, and with patience can be trained to whatever is in their capability. However, some insects are positively dangerous, and great caution must be employed in their handling.

Well, it is for you boys to choose which animals suit your nature and talents as a trainer, and hope-fully the following notes will inform your choice.

Ants

I'll begin by way of a warning and relate that ants can be extremely aggressive if roused to anger. Red ants are particularly dangerous, on account of their poisonous bite, and a gang of them, in an angry mood, can be quite formidable.

By inclination, ants like to live in large assemblages, and they perform at their best in concord with one another. In early circus days numerous attempts were made to train small ant troupes to show in a conventional mixed circus show like our own. However, being prone to sadness and confusion if separated from their community, they tended to give uneven performances and did not make a great attraction for an audience.

Much more successful have been the circuses that showcase ants only. The most famous of these is Seeth & Bidwell's Great Ant Show, which, for more than sixty years now, has toured an ant circus, employing many varieties of black ants and also the more temperamental reds.

As it is impossible to distinguish one from another, ants are the only circus animals that are never given names. In their own community, they are each allotted a number and when performing order themselves accordingly.

Ants love nothing better than to meet together to discuss and decide, and a successful trainer needs to be a good listener and communicator—he or she must possess endless patience, for ant meetings can take considerable time. It is also wise to have an ample quantity of milk to hand, as, in common with many insects, this is their favored food.

Once one has gained their confidence, it is quite a simple matter to train ants to arrange themselves into patterns, as it is a popular pastime for them to do so, particularly when they are young. Circus proprietors have long made use of this natural inclination. In the later part of the nineteenth century, Nathaniel Bidwell, surely _the_ greatest ant trainer of them all, once employed more than fifteen hundred red and black ants in a conical tower that reached over eight hundred feet into the air! (I know this sounds most improbable, but I was a witness to it myself, so I can assure you that it is true.) Perhaps the most remarkable thing about Nat's great achievement was that he alternated rows of black and red ants, and, as you may know, the two have very little regard for each other. One can barely begin to imagine the discussion that must have preceded this outstanding feat.

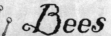

Bees

Bumblebees are affectionate, intelligent animals, they make excellent companions, and, as anybody who has been anywhere near one will have observed, they love to hum. What is not so commonly known is that, given the opportunity, they also love to drum and are capable of keeping time to the most complicated of rhythms. Bees, in all their variety, also love to dance. However, they are not easy to train to anything complicated because of their inability to pay attention for very long.

Their love of music has led humblebees to be taken up by circus bands by way of a mascot, and most circuses will have at least one in the company.

On a cautionary note, it must also be said of bees that they have a sting quite as powerful as a wasp's. However, never in my long years of association with these affable creatures have I ever seen or heard of one actually making use of its weapon.

Now, one might expect to see honeybees as an attraction in the great tent, as they are also popular and friendly creatures. However, due to the unpredictable outcome of their habit of swarming in the spring, coinciding with the start of the tenting season, they have not found a place in the insect circus.

Bombardier Beetles

Bombardier beetles are to be found in circuses all across the land, yet the audience never sees them. Owing to their ability to fire off a volley of burning gas from their bottoms, they are employed to dramatic effect as smoke makers in the circus ring.

These harmless-looking little beetles pack a powerful posterior punch and in the wild can employ their fiery jets to ward off a much larger foe.

Circus folk make use of their marvelous ability to create an atmospheric haze in the arena and, in return for dry quarters and regular meals, the quaint bombardiers seem more than happy to oblige.

Butterflies & Moths

It is a curious fact that only women can train butterflies and moths. This is most probably due to the patience and care taken in their rearing.

Caterpillars are of little use in performance, as they will not take instruction and are forever complaining of hunger. When not feeding they sleep, and although often quite beautiful they do not make a very interesting spectacle. By great contrast, butterflies and moths are sure crowd pleasers. Hand-reared Lepidoptera are totally devoted and loving creatures, and it must be a joy to be carried high into the air in their fond embrace.

Well, boys, I apologize that I can tell you little about butterfly training, but it is women's work and they guard their methods from us men. Perhaps that is to our good fortune, for a butterfly display is the one and only act in the circus that we can admire as an outsider might, with all the wonder that that brings!

Cockchafer

One does not see cockchafers in the circus nowadays, although in the not too distant past chafer baiting was a popular spectacle of a summer's evening.

As a great admirer of animals, I am embarrassed

to relate that my showman predecessors cajoled these hapless creatures into dancing up on their hind legs, in parody of their more agile cousins the racing beetles, by prodding them with sticks or forcing them to walk upon hot coals.

To an ignorant peasantry this must have presented an amusing spectacle, for the 'sport' was practiced over many centuries. Chafer baiting was extremely cruel and has now, mercifully, been outlawed in this country. However, I am reliably informed that this distasteful spectacle can still be witnessed in parts of Germany and Russia.

By inclination, chafers are night creatures and they have seldom found a place within the great tent due to their strong attraction to light. With gentle coercion they can be persuaded to perform a variety of pleasing tricks, but once in front of the glimmer from the lights of circus glowworms they become disorientated and one has the devil's own job of holding them back from harassing their little light-making colleagues.

Crane Flies

Crane flies are delicate, graceful animals and can make a lovely display, all in formation, on a moonlit night. They respond best to a trainer on stilts, for they do not like to talk down to people, and tend to prefer instruction from a female voice, as a male voice is too deep in tone for them to hear. They take instruction well and have remarkably good memories.

Fleas

NO FLEAS, PLEASE

To my certain knowledge, fleas are not now and never have been welcome in reputable insect circuses. They are unsavory creatures who spread malicious rumors, endeavor to create rifts between people, and just love to take a nip at one's ankles!

To call someone a fleabag is a very strong insult within the circus world.

Flies

Although they can be cantankerous and taciturn creatures, flies, in all their variety, are indispensable to the orderly running of a circus, for they invariably fill the post of Agent in Advance. I, in common with the majority of circus owners, have no natural liking for flies and have often wondered how they have been so accepted as a part of circus life. I suspect that their fondness for the sights and smells of the circus environment meant that one or two were always to be found skulking around. What better way to employ them than to send them out in advance of the circus and thereby have them out of the way for most of the week?

An Agent in Advance travels ahead of the circus, arranging suitable tobers and ordering supplies. It is also his job to place posters as advertising.

My young lads, when it comes your time to employ an Agent in Advance, extreme caution is strongly recommended. I believe myself most fortunate in my new agent, Seth Midden, for although he is young and inexperienced he shapes up well and is as keen a fly as ever I've met.

Glowworms & Fireflies

Glowworms and fireflies are neither worm nor fly but are different varieties of beetle. These little creatures have no wings and have difficulty walking. They make up for this sad lack by a wondrous ability to light up the end of their bodies in a most fetching display. It is believed that they do this to attract one another's attention in a "Hello, friend, how do you do?" kind of way.

Glowworms can be temperamental at times. In damp conditions they don't seem to glow so brightly, and when the weather is wet and windy they sometimes refuse to work at all. But they are fairly easy to train and seem to take great pleasure in flashing on and off in time to music.

Curiously, it is only the female glowworms that emit a strong light. The males of the species just have two small lights on their backs and are employed by us in the circus to mark out gangways and fire exits and such like.

Fireflies shine with a much brighter light than their glowworm relatives do. They are natives of tropical Caribbean islands and in Britain have only occasionally been shown in circuses, as they absolutely refuse to perform if the weather is not warm. Due to the unpredictable nature of the British climate, this can be a risky animal to rely on to provide illumination for a circus program.

For my own part, I'll have no dealings with fireflies, as in my experience they tend to a great liking for themselves and a total disregard for others. They are invariably to be found moaning about the vagaries of the English climate, and this can lower the moral of a circus company. However, boys, let me not stand in your way if you are to favor fireflies, for I do believe they will become the modern way to light an arena, once the newfangled heating systems

now being introduced into circus arenas are installed,
for they offer a much stronger light than does the
humbler glowworm.

Ladybug

Ah, the faithful ladybug. What can
I write about him that hasn't been said
a thousand times? Undeniably man's
favorite animal companion, the
ladybug is both an affectionate little
creature and an excellent guard animal. If treated
well they are always joyful and friendly, but
if treated harshly they go to the bad and can become
the very devil to control.

They require little training and will cheerfully
try to do whatever is asked of them if they are
able. As you are well aware, they thrive on affection
and milk, have a terrific sense of humor, and are
peerless in their intelligence and courage.

Liberty Beetles

So named because they never have a rider upon their backs, liberty beetles are always presented in the ring in groups of three, five, seven, or nine, and they tend to be chosen for their color. Although they are aggressive hunters and require constant feeding to pacify them, the sparkling green gardener beetles, with their contrasting red legs and antennae, are the most popular choice.

To dazzling effect, exotic shiny blue and green tropical weevils are also commonly employed as liberties. They are slower to train than gardeners and the need to keep them warm makes them expensive to keep in tiptop condition.

Racing Beetles

Racing beetles are always one variety or another of ground beetle, and again have been associated with man since antiquity. In the circus they are the beetles that acrobatic riders do their tricks upon and are known as rosin-backs, on account of the resin that when applied to the soles of the shoes of the performer stops his feet from slipping.

A good rosin-back must be an even-tempered beetle that can keep a very regular gait. This is of course paramount, for if the beetle were to speed up or slow down it may not be there to land on upon completion of a somersault. As you may imagine, this could have grave consequences for the rider.

Scarab Beetles

Scarab beetles are undeniably the most popular performing beetle, as their balancing abilities make them supreme artistes.

Scarabs were introduced into the circus in the nineteenth century by the intrepid explorer and impresario Margaret "Peggy" Babcock. She discovered them in Morocco's Riff Mountains, where they were employed by the local Scarabin tribe to transport their belongings.

The Scarabin were a nomadic people, and when the time came to move camp they would wrap and bind their possessions into their felt tents, forming a large ball. The scarab beetles would then roll these bundles to the new camping ground.

When not traveling, the beetles had little to do and would amuse themselves by making balls with whatever was at hand and playing with them—rolling them down hills, balancing on them, and other similar amusements. To her enduring credit, Peggy Babcock saw the joy in this pastime and traded a telescope, a pair of sturdy boots, and a metal water bottle for a pair of the finest scarabs. Naming them Dungo and Dunga, she returned with them to London in the autumn of 1818 to a triumphant reception. Every single scarab beetle seen in circuses around the country are descendants of this illustrious pair.

There is no need at all for any kind of training with a scarab, for balancing on a ball is their greatest love. They do thrive on a little flattery, however, so it is wise to be on hand when they are practicing and offer suitable encouragement.

Now, I must warn you, the one slight drawback with keeping female scarabs is their habit of laying their eggs inside one of their rolled bundles. In order that their little ones come into this world undisturbed, these bundles cannot be undone for several weeks, and if a beetle has made use of important costumes or props in the ball's construction, then there can follow an inconvenient wait. A sensible beetle handler will provide the scarab with a suitable quantity of blankets to make her nursery.

Slugs

Since time immemorial, slugs have been used by man as beasts of burden, but as they are stupid creatures and impossible to train, they are not employed by any but the less well off circus managers.

Large tenting circuses invariably favor the popular and much more intelligent snail. It is said of snails that they never forget. As for their cousins the slugs, it can only be said of them that they rarely remember.

Snails

Could there be a circus without snails? It seems almost inconceivable. So much a part of modern circus life, they are peerless at wagon haulage and are keen performers. Snails will do anything asked of them if it is within their capability.

Strange to relate, controversy surrounds the introduction of snails into the circus. When they were first brought to this country more than a hundred years ago, many of the older showmen were suspicious of them. "Insect circus is for insects only," they would say. When it was pointed out that wood lice had always played a part and that they weren't insects either, the old fellows reluctantly changed their minds, and soon the majority of circuses included snails in their company.

Female snails, known as "beauties," are very gentle creatures, but the males, known as "bullies," get very aggressive during the mating season and can become difficult to manage.

The females love to keep company with children and, as I'm sure you are aware, are fond of gossip and chat. Snails have exceptional memories, and it is the custom for circus children to spend time with them, learning from their inestimable knowledge of circus lore and practice.

Since snails are such an essential part of traveling circus life, it may seem churlish to mention their one and only drawback, but drawback it surely is (for some): their slippery trail of slime.

I am happy to relate that the trail does not vex me nearly as much as it once did, for in my capacity as circus owner I ride at the head of the procession when we are traveling. In my youth, I well remember being far back down the line behind many a snail trail, and the slithering and sliding I had to endure can barely be imagined. (Well, I presume it can by you boys, as you must weekly be enduring it yourselves!)

Stag Beetles

Stag beetles are the largest and most fearsome-looking animal to be found in the circus ring. For dramatic effect, it is only the male, with his mighty antlers, that is employed. Despite their enormous size, stag beetles are friendly, gentle creatures and are surprisingly easy to train. An act employing a stag usually involves a duel with a strongman in a bout of wrestling. Although there is an appearance of extreme peril, the handler is in no danger whatsoever.

A stag beetle act invariably ends with the stag vanquished and prostrate upon its back. As with nearly all beetles, this is a position from which they find it extremely difficult to extricate themselves, and assistance is needed from circus hands to right the poor animal before it scuttles offstage to thunderous applause.

Stag beetles are possessors of an enormous appetite, and an Agent in Advance must be sure to order suitable quantities of cakes—their favorite treat— to be available at each new tober.

Wasps

Contained within a strong iron cage, so that they can be no danger to the public, the courageous (or I could say reckless), tamer enters to a fierce buzzing of anger from the entrapped wasps. The very fact that he enters the cage at all is enough of a spectacle for most in the audience, their terror of the awesome creatures being most profound.

Wasps are undeniably <u>the</u> most dangerous animals shown in the circus ring. I cannot stress the importance (if either of you should choose the path of tamer, and I dearly hope that you don't) of keeping a respectful working relationship with a wasp, but at <u>no</u> time can they be trusted!

I must also mention that wasps are carnivores, and it's a gruesome task keeping them well fed. A most unpleasant consequence of their gory diet is their almost constant burping. To find oneself downwind of a foul-smelling wasp belch is an experience not soon forgotten.

Sadly, the pages of insect circus history are littered with tamer fatalities, but, as the spectacle of caged wasps is so enjoyed by the public, many establishments choose to show these malevolent creatures. I am proud to relate that ours does not.

Weevils

Weevils are common performers in all their variety. I've already introduced you to the larger kind, employed in the ring as liberty beetles. Here I'll tell of their tiny cousins, small fry. They are generally considered too little to be seen well in the ring, so are employed by clowns and conjurers in close-up work.

(I know that you already know about these wee fellows, as I have given you some to train, but for the sake of thoroughness I will continue.)

Being both sweet-natured and obedient, small fry are often the first animals that a circus child might attempt to train, and a lot of valuable experience can be gained from working with these harmless little creatures.

Wood Lice

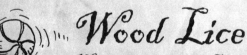

With great affection, I will now make mention of the humble and ever faithful wood lice.

These most engaging of little characters obviously need no introduction to you, as they have been man's constant companion since time immemorial.

Long associated with clowns and clowning, wood lice love to curl up into a ball, and however hard one throws one away, it will always cheerfully return. Clowns employ this characteristic to very comical effect, juggling and rolling the little animals back and forth between them.

There cannot be many a household that does not have a wood louse as a pet, and there can hardly be a child in the land who has not attempted to teach one a few simple tricks.

Worms

Wild earthworms have long been a curse to traveling circuses, as they have a habit of disrupting a show by popping their heads up, right in the middle of the circus ring, during a performance. It has long been believed that they do this because they are attracted to the music of the circus band.

This assumption has recently been born out by the arrival, from the exotic East, of the novel and extremely popular worm charmers of Rajasthan. In India, the practice of charming worms goes back many centuries. It's a common sight at fairs and markets all across the land to see a worm emerge from a basket and reach its head high into the air as it sways and 'dances' to the sinuous music of a strolling piper or a small brass band.

Due to the popularity of this novel and pleasing attraction, and the rareness of Indian worm charmers in this country, attempts have been made by circus colleagues to charm our native worms. To my certain knowledge no success has yet been achieved, and as I'm sure you are aware worms cannot talk, so it's not a lot of good consulting them on the matter.

Perhaps you boys might discover the secret of charming worms? I would be a very proud father if you did so, and can happily imagine what a grand attraction it would add to our circus!

So there we have it, and, as I said, the choice is yours. But remember, whichever creatures you decide upon, to make sure you treat them kindly. For if you do they'll reward you with a long succession of successful insect circus seasons.

Your loving father,

George Piper, Esq.

November 1858

Sylvia

Art

Rufus

Bill & the Bombardiers

Eliza Piper

Chester

Noah

Sgt. Sergeant

Seth Midden

Vince Midden

Jasper